MERCY MORE THAN LIFE

FuzionPress
Burnsville, MN

MERCY MORE THAN LIFE

Ethel "Sally" Blaine Millett, WWII Bataan Nurse and Japanese POW

MEG BLAINE CORRIGAN

First Edition
Printed in the United States of America

Paperback ISBN: 978-1-955541-74-9
eBook ISBN: 978-1-955541-76-3
Hardcover ISBN: 978-1-955541-75-6
LCCN: Pending

Cover design and interior design by Ann Aubitz
Headshot by Hilda Birdie Photography

Cover photo of nurses liberated by Lt. Col. Helen Hennessey
Lt. Col. Helen Hennessey was captured as a prisoner of war in 1942 and sent to the Santo Tomas internment camp in Manila. She was one of the many nurses captured on the island of Corregidor. This is an image of many of those nurses being rescued when Santo Tomas was eventually liberated by American troops in 1945. [12 February 1945]

Images in the book are photos from the Ethel "Sally" Blaine Millett Collection, unless marked otherwise.

Published by
FuzionPress
1250 E 115th Street
Burnsville, MN 55337
612-781-2815
FuzionPress.com

Oh beautiful for heroes proved
in liberating strife,
who more than self did country love
and **mercy more than life***,*
America, America, let God thy gold refine,
and all success be nobleness
and every grace be Thine.

America the Beautiful
Verse 3
by Katharine Lee Bates

The stars from your flag
were scattered
all over your casket,
and we knew you were there,
dancing with those stars,
your spirit free for eternity.

In Loving Memory of My Aunt
Ethel "Sally" Blaine Millett

INTRODUCTION

How would you like to have someone drop a book idea in your lap, along with literally BOXES of information to help you write it? And how would you like to find out, soon after, that the protagonist for this book left a two-hour oral history that would make up a large part of this book in detail, so all that would be left would be the history and context of the story, which could easily be found on the Internet? Add my own "spin" and some dialogue, and the story would be complete! An author's dream! And this is exactly how this book came into being.

Let me elaborate.

My entire life, I knew my dad's sister, my Aunt Ethel Blaine Millett (who was later nicknamed "Sally"), was a war hero. It was much later in life that I got to know and appreciate Sally. She passed away in 2004, and I met my cousin Van Millett and his wife, Ann, in Washington, DC, when I attended Sally's memorial service at Arlington National Cemetery. Sally was buried on top of her late husband, as is the custom at these rapidly filling sacred national burial grounds. Several years later, in 2017, my cousin Van passed away from a similar condition that took his father at a young age. His widow, Ann, contacted me some time after Van's death and asked me if I would like Aunt Sally's vast collection of newspaper articles, telegrams, photographs, and memorabilia. I immediately said someone closer to Sally would undoubtedly want the materials more than I. But Ann assured me that she had checked with the relatives, and no one in the immediate family was interested in Sally's papers. (Since that time, I have made an exhaustive, unsuccessful effort to contact other family members to see if anyone more closely related to Sally would want her papers.)

When Ann contacted me, I immediately booked a flight from my home near St. Paul, Minnesota, to San Antonio, Texas, where Sally had lived the last number of years of her life and where her papers were waiting for me at Ann Millett's home. Ann and I staged the boxes in her dining area, and I began opening boxes of mostly seventy-five-year-old papers. I didn't think to bring some antihistamines, and I sneezed my head off for four days going through the materials, many over seventy years old, while Ann was at work. I boxed up what I wanted, tossed duplicates, and spent way too much money shipping the boxes home. I boarded my return flight to Minneapolis, dreaming of starting "Sally's book" as soon as the airplane wheels hit the ground in Minnesota. Unsurprisingly, life got in the way of my dreams of beginning to write. Surgeries, hospitalizations, a cancer scare, a little thing called the coronavirus, cancer in a family member, and a contentious divorce all took away my time, my motivation, and occasionally my sanity. Starting the book was delayed for several years until late 2024, when I began seriously working on the first draft.

My father had told me that Sally had recorded an oral history at what used to be the Nemitz Museum in Fredericksburg, Texas, near San Antonio. I called to find out more and learned that the facility was now called the National Museum of the Pacific War. I spoke with museum staff member Chris McDougal and learned that all the participants who have recorded oral histories, including Aunt Sally, have signed a release form so that anyone in the United States is welcome to listen to, copy, and even publish their oral histories in part or in full. Furthermore, each oral history has been converted into a written transcript that anyone in the US may also use. I could write much of the story in Sally's own words, from her perspective. This gift just keeps on giving!

I am a Christian author, speaker, and trainer. In approaching Sally's story, I was certain I wanted to include a message from and about Christ. I knew my aunt was a woman of faith. But Sally's oral history proved to be more about the day-to-day, secular aspects of her time in the Philippines, with little to no reporting of matters of spirituality. So, I created the character of a young Filipino man, Angelito, who speaks truth to the nurses and sings their praises. The nurses never thought of themselves as heroes. Indeed, they humbly performed their wartime field duties as if they still worked in Stotsenberg Army Hospital and were not suffering unimaginable hardships, first in temporary open-air hospitals and then in a POW camp. No one else gave the nurses any special credit or treatment in such a profound way as Angelito because everyone was just trying to survive. The nurses who became known as the "Angels of Bataan" were literally being celebrated in my book mostly by a fictitious character whose name, not coincidentally, was "Angel" in Spanish.

Note: The experiences Sally told during her oral history are one hundred percent true. Many other sources have corroborated her telling of the Bataan campaign and her internment in the prisoner-of-war (POW) camp. The storyline of the character Angelito and his interactions with the nurses and other hospital staff and patients is purely fictional. In addition, I have inserted dialogue and embellished the physical detail, mood, and dialogue in many other scenes to give the story more depth.

So come with me on a unique journey you may have never even known about (especially those of you who do not personally remember much about World War II and the Philippines). You will be amazed at the courage and dedication of my Aunt Sally and her fellow Army and Navy nurses and Filipino medical staff who survived the Bataan jungle, were captured by the Imperial forces of Japan, and spent nearly three years in a prisoner-of-war (POW) camp inside the walls of what had been a Jesuit university. You will marvel at the ways these nurses helped assemble and operate hospitals with limited supplies and equipment, facing danger by the hour but keeping up the spirits of their patients during the most trying conditions imaginable.

Seventy-seven American nurses were captured, and seventy-seven American nurses came home. A miracle indeed!

I'll see you on the other side, where I provide an Epilogue and some questions for you to answer yourself or discuss with your book club or your family or friends. There will be plenty of material to talk about!

A HISTORY LESSON AT A FAMILY REUNION

Our family didn't see much of Sally or her children when my sister and I were growing up. My father was a career Air Force officer, and we moved every three years or so when he got transferred to a new place. So, in 2000, when my parents went one last time to the Blaine Family Reunion near Bible Grove in northeastern Missouri—where it all started—I arranged to meet them there. Sally was there too, and she rode in a rental car with my parents and me from northeast Missouri to Kansas City to catch our planes home: her to San Antonio, Texas; my parents to Las Vegas, Nevada; and me to New Brighton, Minnesota.

Sally had always been a reverent mystery to me. She was a beautiful, regal-looking woman with soft, light brown hair and brown eyes, whose behavior did not hint at the trauma she had endured. Her conversations with others, with her curated southern drawl, seemed "normal" enough to me. As a child, I was so in awe of her, I would not have approached her to have a conversation just between us. But at family gatherings, as she interacted with her brothers and sisters, her own sons, nieces and nephews, and never-ending relatives that surely made up most of the population of Scotland County, Missouri, I realized that she *was* every bit as normal as all the other folks I was akin to.

The night before our planes departed from that last reunion, we ate a late supper in the hotel restaurant and said our goodnights in the hallway. My parents went into their room, and Aunt Sally and I walked toward our respective rooms.

"Why don't you come to my room to visit?" she asked. "I'd like to hear about what's going on in your life."

"I'd love that," I said. "But only if you'll tell me your story, because I've never heard it from you..."

"Of course," she said.

And I stayed in her room and listened to her story...until four o'clock in the morning.

PROLOGUE

The Rising Sun Flag
(Japanese: 旭日旗 *Kyokujitsu-ki*)

THE EMPEROR HAD NO CHOICE

The Abyss hissed. The emperor ignored it. For now. Michinomiya Hirohito remembered the day his father died at age forty-nine, in 1926. Hirohito was barely a man, only twenty-five years old. His father, Emperor Taisho, had not been well most of his life. When he was three weeks old, he suffered an attack of spinal meningitis, which affected his ability to walk, as well as his mental capacity. He was unable to speak well, and his ability to think critically and make good decisions was never developed. He became reclusive and acted oddly for a member of the Japanese dynasty. These limitations plagued Taisho all his life, requiring much supervision and grooming from the royal court to render him suitable for his role as emperor. The grooming was not successful. Finally, he went into full retirement in 1919.

At the age of eighteen, Hirohito was made prince regent, not fully a head of state, but able to lead the government because his father could not. Conflict, always conflict! The young prince just wanted to be left alone, to travel and study, and learn about amazing things in the world. When his father finally died, Hirohito became emperor, whether he liked it or not. He had been the first

Japanese crown prince to study abroad, pursuing his interest in marine biology—not exactly a skill he could use in leading an emerging Asian nation. Hirohito had seen Western culture, and his return to the rigors of Japanese royalty was uncomfortable at best, tortuous too.

Now at his father's death in 1926, here Hirohito was, no longer the reluctant heir to the throne, but supposedly solidly in the role of emperor for life. He wondered, from time to time, if he had somehow inherited his father's difficulties, like the inability to lead a nation sensibly or to fend off the emotional toll the role would take on him. He was not of a military mindset, but he was required to watch the reviews of all the men in uniform, marching in goosestep, heads turned toward the young man who was now their leader. Why did they need such a formidable military anyway? Hirohito had moments when he felt unworthy of this responsibility, surreptitiously thrust upon him. There was no escaping his place now, and he wished his father had been more of a mentor to him. But the prince knew very early that his father was not going to have any deep connections to him or his three brothers. And there was no one else around to guide him in the way a functioning father might. Hirohito feared his own dark side and didn't understand his deep feelings. Though Hirohito's word was essentially the law of the land, Japanese culture viewed the emperor as a divine being who did not get involved with the messy business of politics.

The Abyss hissed again. That unseen, unexpected cavern of pure evil that taunted young Hirohito until he feared he might tumble right down into the void. He suspected he might collide with his darker self someday, like the icebergs he had heard about in faraway waters, where colossal frozen masses showed just their tips, but underneath the waterline, a dark and deadly mass was lurking.

Hirohito did not know, when his father died and he became emperor, that fifteen years later, he would try unsuccessfully to be marginally involved with his military leaders. But they would persuade him that diplomacy was not the way mighty Japanese emperors were to approach things. Japan was to become part of the Axis, they told him: Hitler, Mussolini, and Hirohito. "The emperor seemed at ease and unshakable once he had made a decision," Japanese Prime Minister Hideki Tojo was quoted as saying. "If His Majesty had any regret, he would have looked somewhat grim." But that hadn't happened. "There was no such indication, which must be a result of his determination," Tojo said in a memo. "I'm completely relieved. Given the current conditions, I could say we have practically won (World War II) already."

Hirohito eventually gave his tacit approval to his nation's plans for December 7, 1941, when just before eight o'clock in the morning, 350 Japanese planes supported by submarines, battleships, and destroyers would attack Pearl Harbor, Hawaii. A total of 2,403 people would die in that attack, in which Japan would destroy nineteen American ships lined up in the harbor in precise rows, like ducks in a bathtub. The ships would include the USS Arizona, which would end up lying quietly at the bottom of the harbor, cradling 900 souls for eternity.

And Hirohito would also approve the "Other Pearl Harbor," just eighteen hours later when the Japanese forces would invade the Philippine Islands, working their way southward to bomb Clark Air Base on Luzon Island, forty miles north of the capital of Manila. Clark would be one of many targets that day. There, a young nurse in the barracks would stoop to tie her shoe, suddenly feeling the percussion of the bombs. Time would slow to a crawl. She would look out the window and see the flash of light, and then she would hear the great bombs falling and fighter planes strafing the motionless American aircraft as each in turn was obliterated. The young nurse and the emperor were both to be remembered after that terrible day, for very different reasons.

Now, Hirohito wished the darkness would depart from him. He turned away from the Abyss and tried to tell himself it wasn't there at all.

But he could still hear it hissing as he walked away. "Axis of Power!" it whispered. "Axis!"

PART I

Ethel ("Sally"), center left, age six, cutting up
Photo from the Ethel "Sally" Blaine Millett Collection

AN ANGEL IN THE MAKING

"Ethel!" her mother called sharply. "You get in this house right now! I am losing patience!"

Ethel was eight years old. Her slender body leaned over the tall milkweed next to the beginning of the woods by her family's front yard. Her long chestnut hair was even close enough to catch the feathery stalks.

"I'm comin', Mama. I'm catching butterflies!"

"Listen to me, girl! Get away from that tall grass and those weeds! They are full of chiggers!"

"Just a minute!" she hollered impatiently, holding up a glass jelly jar she had liberated from her mother's cupboard. "I've almost just about caught another one of these butterflies!"

Small child, Preserver of Monarch Butterflies, kind to all creatures. But with a warrior's heart, facing a yet-unknown world of unimaginable challenges. Just one more butterfly!

"Ethel Lenore, I am NOT telling you again!" Her mother smacked her hands together over the trash can to remove the flour she was using to fix fried chicken. She grabbed a towel to wipe her hands off—and maybe just to give that child a swat on her behind—and headed out the back door.

Ethel saw her mother. She let the butterfly she had in a jar go free and turned toward the house.

"Lord, child, why DON'T you come when I call you?"

"Mama, all these pretty Monarch butterflies try to eat the milkweed but some of them get stuck in the plant parts. I help them get out so they can fly free, all the way to Mexico!"

"Yes, well, chiggers like to sit on those milkweed stalks too, and you are going to find out the hard way that chiggers like to drive you crazy in the night when they bore into your skin, and you start to itching!"

Sally wasn't always called Sally. That nickname came later. She was born Ethel Lenore Blaine, in February of 1915, at the home of her parents, Alta Hunter Blaine and William Blaine, in a tiny town called Bible Grove in northeast Missouri. The Blaines were crop farmers and livestock owners, and Ethel was the tenth of thirteen children. And what a lineup! Those Blaine children had so many different personalities, Ethel sometimes thought her parents' household was like living in the Lincoln Park Zoo in Chicago, which Ethel heard about in her school. In Ethel's imagination, each of her brothers and sisters was like a different animal with different behaviors and temperaments. Ethel loved them all, but they struck her as many very different kids in such a big family.

From the time she was small, Ethel seemed to be wise for her years. She listened intently to everything around her: people, animals, the weather, news of the outside world that she overheard when her daddy spoke of it, and impending explosions from her mother when Ethel disobeyed. She wasn't afraid to comment about anything going on in their household or on the Blaine farm, whether her opinion was asked for or not. This led to many interesting exchanges with her parents and her older siblings. But Ethel still engaged anyone and everyone in her ongoing quest to learn all about the world around her and beyond the family farm and the tiny town of Bible Grove, Missouri.

"ETHEL," the woman said. "This is the LAST time I'm going to call you in! Supper is almost on the table!"

"Okay, Mama! I'm coming!"

Missouri winters are not unbearable when compared with the more northern states in what is called the Midwest part of the United States. But in the early part of the 20th century when Ethel was born, even small amounts of snowfall needed to be cleared by hand and with *snow rollers*. These were heavy wheels pulled by horses that compacted the snow into a level, compressed surface that people, animals, and vehicles could travel on. "Snow days" where everything shut down, including school, were rare when Ethel was a child. But like children everywhere, the Blaine kids loved to play in the snow and have snowball fights. If enough snow fell, they would build forts, make snow slides, and take their sleds to slide on one of the many hills surrounding the Blaine farm.

The summers could be brutal. It was not unusual for the temperatures to reach the mid to high 90s with humidity running close to suffocating, making summers oppressive and uncomfortable for humans and livestock. Heavy rainfall and area droughts kept farmers guessing what Mother Nature would bring next. But the farm work had to be done, rain or shine, hot or cold. And the Blaine kids helped with some aspects of the operation from the time they could stand up.

As if the heat and humidity weren't enough torture in the summer, every member of the family learned about the chiggers one way or another. Alta Blaine was smart to watch when her young children got too close to the wooded area around the front of the farm where chiggers clung to grass blades and milkweed pods. Almost invisible, microscopic chigger larvae attach to people's clothing and then jump to their skin. A liquid chemical is released from the insects to kill skin cells. The dead cells make a sort of straw with which the chiggers drink live skin tissue. The chemical causes intense itching that can make life miserable for up to two weeks. But the chiggers themselves will fall off the host's skin once they drink their fill. Like tiny summer vampires, they invade tall grasses and moist riverbanks and children's dreams.

"Ethel! You mind your mama, now! Stay out of that high grass, or you'll be layin' awake tonight scratchin' those chiggers!"

The children attended a school in town, about two miles from the farm. Ethel's daddy owned some spotted ponies named Dick and Sadie. Her dad didn't like Dick's stubbornness, and he thought Sadie was lazy. Ethel's brother Mayhue was six years older than Ethel, and he usually drove the ponies.

"Dick can count to six," Ethel said one day.

"What makes you think that?" Mayhue asked her.

"Because," Ethel replied, "there are six of us kids, and the minute little Madeline gets one foot into the wagon and grabs the handle to pull herself up, Dick takes off!"

Dick would walk on his hind legs for twenty or thirty feet, dragging poor Sadie along before she knew what hit her. Sadie could never keep up with Dick.

There was a barn next to the school, and the horses stayed there while classes were in session. The story went that, when the boys grew up and left home, their dad didn't think the girls could handle the ponies, so then they walked two miles to school instead.

A few years later, when Ethel was a teenager, her daddy bought a small horse named Ribbon. She was a chunky little horse, dapple gray with a dark mane and tail. One day their dad was talking to the neighbor.

"I really got my money's worth with that little mare," William Blaine said. "She's worthless because she's 'barn sour,' and none of my kids can get her to go very far from home."

"How's that?" asked the neighbor.

"Well," William said, "when she thinks she's gone far enough, Ribbon just turns around and heads back to the barn. No amount of pulling on the reins or kicking her sides or even using a switch will make her behave."

But Ethel liked Ribbon, and one day she managed to ride the little mare bareback all the way to her aunt and uncle's house fourteen miles away. It took Ethel half the day to get there, even when she was able to make Ribbon gallop, which was not the horse's favorite gait. Ethel rode from Bible Grove cross country through the neighbors' fields she knew like the back of her hand. The day was sunny, hot, and sultry. A baby blue sky hung high above her, except for the tufts of developing rain clouds far in the distance along the horizon. When the fields gave way to some large woods, Ethel followed a bright, bubbling stream down toward the river. She knew she had to follow the Fabius River into town so she could cross on the new car bridge. Her cousin's family lived on a farm on the outskirts of Memphis.

When she got to her relatives' farm, she saw her cousin Geraldine shucking sweet corn outside the back door of the house.

"Hey, Jerri," Ethel said, "how'd you like to climb on and go for a little ride?"

Jerri complied, putting down the corn she was shucking, assuming she'd be back in a few minutes. She used Ethel's foot as a step to boost herself up onto Ribbon, and she settled in behind her cousin.

But after a short distance in the wrong direction, Ribbon had had enough of these girls' foolishness. That horse took off at a dead run and went right straight back to the safety of her barn on the Blaine farm. The girls jumped off the little horse right before she went through the barn door, which almost knocked the two of them off the horse. Ribbon was winded, running that far at full speed, but she seemed almost proud of herself for outmaneuvering the two girls.

Nobody ever said how Geraldine got back home, but Ethel got into some real trouble with her mother when she and Cousin Jerri showed up at the Blaine farm after supper and darn near dark.

Bible Grove had a nice school for such a small town. No one-room schoolhouse for the Blaine children! Their dad was a school board member most of his adult life, chairing the board from time to time. Bible Grove School boasted a two-story brick building with a cafeteria in the basement, an auditorium upstairs with a raised stage and a curtain that could be drawn open and closed. The building had several classrooms, one for each grade.

One day Ethel's fifth-grade teacher was giving a lesson on world geography and Ethel thought she had identified her own special paradise.

"When I grow up," she told the teacher after class, "I'm going to the Philippines!"

Ethel probably didn't realize that the Philippine Islands were halfway around the world from Bible Grove, Missouri. And it's for sure that she didn't know what the Philippine Islands would mean for her at the start of World War II.

GIRL TO HERO

It was never exactly clear why Ethel decided to travel eighteen hundred miles to attend nurses' training in San Diego, California, when there were plenty of options closer to home. Some said Ethel was avoiding a particular young farm boy who insisted she marry him. Ethel did not like him, and she made it clear.

"He has a sharp nose and a weak chin!" she exclaimed. "His hair sticks out everywhere and he walks with a hitch in his gitalong. I can't imagine what his children would look like. Their mama would have to tie a pork chop around each of their necks jus' so the dawg would play with them. I don't want any babies that look like him, and I don't want to be a farm wife!"

In spite of the boy's obvious affection for Ethel, she would never be mean and tell him how she really felt. But she continued to complain about him at home.

"I've seen how much work farming is," she told her sisters, "and us kids have heard Mama and Daddy talking about how tight money is all the time. I say, 'no thanks' to farming!"

Others said Ethel was being her typical risk-taker. But maybe her childhood dream of living in a tropical paradise led Ethel to take the four-day-long train ride to San Diego. In 1936, she began the nursing program at the San Diego County Hospital, a three-year program that included experience in charge (lead) nursing, pharmaceuticals, direct (in home) patient care of poor patients in the county's custody, and private patient care at Mercy Hospital.

Ethel grew into her young adult self gracefully. She made friends easily, worked hard, and excelled in her nurses' training. She began to take special care with her looks. Gone were the "bowl" haircuts her mother gave to her and her brothers and sisters in the family kitchen. Ethel was now getting her locks trimmed and styled in a glamorous beauty shop with ladies of all walks of life. And she also began wearing makeup, learning from some of the other young women in her dormitory how to apply it for the most impact. Ethel's fellow students—all women— came from all over the United States and spoke of many different experiences from the ones Ethel had in rural northeastern Missouri.

"Wait," said one young woman from New York City, "you mean there really is a town called '*Bible Grove*?' I thought you were kidding!"

"Yes, there is," said Ethel in her Missouri drawl, "and it's about as far from New York City as a place can get and still be on this planet!"

All the students laughed at that.

"I *love* your southern accent!" a student from Michigan exclaimed. "Do you all talk like that all the time, or just for show?"

More laughter.

"I beg your pardon," Ethel said. "Of *course* we talk like this all the time! It's perfectly natural for us 'cause it's the way we *learned* to talk."

Ethel (Sally) At Nursing School Graduation, 1939
Photo from the Ethel "Sally" Blaine Millett Collection

Ethel finished her training in the fall of 1939. She had been inspired by her two older brothers' entry into military service. Millard was an army enlistee who worked as a mechanic, and Mayhue was an Army Air Corps pilot. An older brother, Orin, had enlisted in the army during World War I but died in the Spanish Flu pandemic before he ever left boot camp. Ethel wanted to follow in her brothers' honorable footsteps. From Mercy Hospital, Ethel went to Letterman Hospital near San Francisco and joined the Army Nurse Corps.

From the time it opened in 1899, Letterman Hospital (previously Army General Hospital at the Presidio) had state-of-the-art technology and equipment, a telephone system, and primitive X-ray machines. The facility opened its doors to victims of northern California earthquakes and fires. In 1901, Letterman made headlines when the facility became the first army general hospital to employ women of the newly created Army Nurse Corps.

In November of 1940, when twenty-five-year-old Ethel reported for her first duty as an Army Nurse Corps member, most of the patients Letterman Hospital saw were soldiers who were going to or from active duty in various places of the globe. One of the first things Ethel noticed at the hospital was a sign-up sheet at the bottom of a stairwell asking for nurses interested in going to the Philippines. There was a pencil on a string to use for signing up.

"I put my name on that list *three times*," she told a fellow nurse. "And each time, the list goes down and they don't get ahold of me."

The next time a new sign-up sheet was posted, Ethel happened to have a pen in her hand. She thought maybe if she signed her name in pen and all the others were in pencil, hers might get noticed. And it worked!

But Ethel's commanding officer, Miss Near, wanted to have a word with her.

"You mean you *want* to go to the *Philippines?*" she asked.

"Yes, I do!"

"Do you have any idea what it's like over there?" Miss Near asked. Miss Near had been to the Philippines for more than one tour of duty, so she knew what was to be expected.

Ethel was slightly taken aback. She envisioned some sort of natives storming around in costumes and trying to raid the hospital there. She knew the hospital was on an army base, but she wondered exactly what Miss Near was thinking of.

"Well, no, I guess I don't really know," she answered quietly.

"Honey, you're going to have to work very hard if you go there."

Ethel's answer was swift. "Well," she said, "has anyone ever told you that I'm lazy?"

"Oh, no," Miss Near replied. "But I just want to assure you it's not going to be easy if you go over there."

Ethel did not ask Miss Near why she thought it would be so hard. But with talk of war throughout the world at the time, Ethel had a feeling that Miss Near knew more than she was letting on about the troop buildup and preparations for possible conflict. Ethel convinced Miss Near that she was serious about the assignment. Miss Near completed the necessary paperwork transferring the young nurse to Stotsenburg Hospital north of Manila, and Ethel was on her way to realizing her childhood dream of seeing the Philippines.

WEST TO THE TROPICS

The morning fog was lifting across the San Francisco Bay as the troop ship left the marina and headed west toward the open Pacific Ocean. It was August 1941. Ethel stood outdoors at the railing on the port side with her soft brown hair blowing in the ocean breeze. She was unable to identify her mood, or moods. She was simultaneously feeling excited, scared, teary-eyed, slightly panicked, and a little bit crazy. It seemed like only yesterday she had graduated from her nursing program, and although she had confidence in her clinical training and experience, she still had a bit of that farm girl in her. She thought of her mother now, how hard her mother cried when her sisters helped her load her baggage onto the train in Missouri. How far from home California had seemed, and now...now she was taking a seventeen-day voyage to Manila, nearly seven thousand miles from San Francisco. Remembering Miss Near's inquisition of her—"You are going to have to work *very hard* if you go over there"—Ethel thought, *Can it be harder than farm work? What if I can't hold up?*

The Presidio's fortress stood sentinel, as it had since 1776, as if saluting the young army nurse as she passed.

The Golden Gate Bridge, built just eleven years before, shone in the morning sun like a steel rainbow in a sky of misty blue. The fog was almost gone by the time the ship passed under the bridge. A crew member used the massive horns to play a short tune, just showing off for the tourists driving over the bridge. And soon, the bridge, the Presidio, the Bay, and California were just a distant recollection. The open sea roiled around the troop ship as if to say, "Ethel, you are now in uncharted territory!"

Ethel soon met other nurses who were heading for Manila.

"Say," she asked a group of the other nurses one day, "did any of you get grilled by Miss Near about how tough life would be in the Philippines?"

"I did," said a short blonde woman wearing a stylish sun bonnet.

"Me too!" said a couple of other nurses.

"And," Ethel continued, "did Miss Near ask any of you why *you* thought you were suited for the tough job ahead."

The few who had talked to the head nurse had been asked if they were up to the task, but most just found their names on the list to make the trip. Now the ones who hadn't been singled out by Miss Near *really* wondered what they had gotten themselves into!

The young women made fast friends, playing shuffleboard and card games on the ship's deck. Others made it a point to keep to themselves, reading and sleeping on deck.

PART II

GALLEONS ON TRADE WINDS

The first ships to reach the Philippines from the east were four galleons in 1564, when Spaniard Miquel Lopez de Legaspi led an expedition. Legaspi claimed both Guam and the Philippines for King Philip II of Spain. Thus began a 250-year-long galleon trade, during which both island nations were introduced to the Catholic Church and the Spanish language and culture. The galleons carried spices from the island nations and returned with many goods and products never seen in the two countries. When the United States defeated Spain in the Spanish-American War in 1898, Spain ceded the Philippines to the United States as part of the treaty ending the war. The Philippines remained an American protectorate, with the intention to transition to full independence on July 4, 1946.

The Philippine archipelago includes 7,640 islands. Its inhabitants speak as many as 187 different languages, mainly of the Malayo-Polynesian language family. Together with Spanish and English, the spoken dialects make up a crazy quilt of speech on any given day. Most Filipinos speak English, so the nurses did not have to worry about being understood by native hospital workers, shopkeepers, and other residents of the island nation. Because English was so prevalent, it is doubtful any of the nurses learned even a fraction of the local dialects. They did not have time for such endeavors.

Pre–World War II troop ships, like the one on which these nurses traversed the Pacific Ocean, often began life as commercial ocean liners. They were leased by the Department of the Navy or, when necessary, were conscripted—forced—into service. The ships were immediately painted dull gray, inside and out, top to bottom. Then the ships were outfitted with a minimal amount of armament, but these vessels were not expected to see combat. The ocean liners were faster than the ships used for other purposes by any navy in the world. Capable of moving many troops very quickly for their time, they could also outrun submarines and enemy cruisers. Although the ships were known for their impressive speed, seventeen days seemed like an eternity to the nurses going to the Philippines. The length of time it took a troop ship to sail from the western shores of the United States to the Philippines would play prominently in how the Americans responded when the military personnel (including the Army Nurse Corps members) were in dire need of rescuing.

FLOWERS, FUN, AND A FILIPINO BUS DRIVER

Ethel's troopship traveled on a centuries-old commerce route. Soft trade winds and gentle currents made easy work for the sailors most of the time. At first, the nurses were shy and didn't want to draw attention to themselves from the ship's crew. But as the Pacific days stayed sunny and warm, even on the open seas, the nurses began to appear outside in smaller and smaller pieces of clothing. Finally, the bathing suits came out, the hair got pinned up off their faces, and the girls were on full display for the grateful all-male crew.

The nurses changed ships in Honolulu, and they had a chance to try out their land legs for a few hours. Their trip was nearly half over, and the next stop would be Manila. People in Honolulu told them that the Philippines looked much like Hawaii: a group of islands with white sand beaches, swaying palm trees, abundant flowers, and lush, green forests. It was hard to get back on the ship after their brief stay in Honolulu, but they had more of an idea how beautiful the Philippine Islands would be.

And they were not disappointed.

The army bus that pulled up alongside the troop ship in Port Manila was painted a gloomy shade of olive green, the signature color of all army vehicles. A destination tag on the front of the bus said: Stotsenburg Hospital, which was located forty miles northwest of Manila. While the nurses assigned to Stotsenburg said their goodbyes to others headed to different hospitals, several men materialized suddenly to transfer the women's baggage from the ship to the bus. The men moving the bags seemed to be under the direction of a young Filipino man in army fatigues with Filipino military patches on the chest and the sleeves. Soon, the buses were all loaded, and the nurses could see the bustling activity in the busy port as they waited to get underway. The young Filipino man also turned out to be their bus driver. He climbed into the bus, closed the door, and lifted a microphone out of its holder with one hand as he started the engine with the other. The gears ground and they were on their way.

"Helloooooooo, ladeezzz!" he cried into a crackling speaker system. "My name is *Angelito*. My first name means 'little angel or message from God.' The night I was born, my mother, she saw the Blessed Virgin Mary through the window of our home, this is true family story, and she gave me a special name. My mother is like a saint to me. She lives in Manila, with my younger sister. My father has been gone many years. I write to my mother once a week.

"Filipino peoples place great pride in the names our parents give us. My middle name is Domingo, 'of the Lord.'

My last name? Orasyon-Del Rosario. Orasyon is my mother's...how you say? Name before finding husband?"

"Maiden name!" came the answer in a chorus of female voices.

"Yes, yes. Maiden name," said Angelito. "Orasyon means 'prayer,' Orasyon, and the next name means 'of the rosary,' Del Rosario. So altogether, my name means 'angel or message from God, of the Lord, prayer, of the rosary.' Angelito Domingo Orasyon-Del Rosario."

He tapped his chest for emphasis. "I am Catholic and I travel with Christ. Welcome to our peaceful island paradise where our God looks with favor on us each day!" He kissed a crucifix hanging on a chain around his neck. "I am grateful to my God for everything I have, and I try to help other people travel with Christ.

"And now, on behalf of the Filipino people, I wish to welcome you and offer you some excellent observances as we drive to Clark Field, Stotsenberg Hospital, and the modern barracks you will be living in. The hospital is located on the Clark Army Base in Pampanga, about fifty miles north of our capital of Manila."

The bus went through the main gate of the Port Manila grounds, and soon the views from the windows were much more enticing than the shipyard.

"What's that beautiful purple flower climbing up that iron fence over there?" one of the nurses asked.

"That," said Angelito, "is bougainvillea, a beautiful native plant that thrives here year-round. But, ladeezzz, you have seen nothing yet! I will take you on...how you say? ...whirling winds tour of our wonderful island of Luzon and the city of Manila. I will show you the excellent happiness of Ayala Triangle Gardens, Mehan Gardens, Dolomite Beach, and many top-rate buildings for your looking pleasure, such as Coconut Palace, Roman Santos Building…"

Angelito was an enticing guide, and soon the nurses were listening to his patter and relaxing in their seats. The trip to Manila on the troop ship was long and often boring, and the city sights were a welcome change from the wide-open ocean.

Suddenly a building a block from their route caught Ethel's eye. She shuddered at the sight of it, though she obviously knew nothing about it.

"What is that walled compound over there?" she asked, pointing out her bus window.

"That," said Angelito, with a flourish, "is the Pontifical and Royal University of Santo Tomas, built in 1611 when our country was a territory of Spain. We call it Catholic University of the Philippines. It was originally allowed to train young men for the priesthood. But now it is a university with thousands enrolled and many types of teaching. It is the oldest Pontifical college in Asia and has offered the courses all the time except in 1898 and 1899 during the Philippine Revolution against Spain. The walls completely surround the forty-acre campus, and it has a center garden for prayer and meditation…"

"It looks creepy," Ethel said to herself, shuddering again. She looked back at the receding university campus, which seemed as if it was rising out of its foundation and…*groaning*.

Ethel did not know that the Abyss, even now, was beginning to overtake this sacred community of higher learning, and the enemy was coming to invade that compound.

And Ethel never suspected that the evil the Abyss held would someday try to capture her and her fellow nurses as they risked their very lives to care for their charges.

The Abyss hissed, but the nurses' bus was hurtling along toward their new lives as army nurses in paradise. They didn't hear a thing except the chatter of the bus driver, Angelito.

REALITY CHECK

When the bus pulled into the main gates of Clark Field, the nurses began to get an idea what a large complex they were being assigned to. Their Filipino driver, Angelito, told them that the base was originally called Fort Stotsenburg, named after a US Captain, who was killed in combat in the Philippines in 1899. Angelito called out each area they passed by.

"There are three parade grounds," Angelito told the nurses, "all on the west end of the base. The telephone exchange building over to our right serves as both a post office and for housing the operators for telephone connections. The railway station, over on the left, is a very important place to know, because that's how you gonna get to Manila for the nightlife!" Angelito laughed heartily. "Oh, you don't want to miss out on the night life! It is like something you never see before! Trust me, ladies, I tell you the God's truth."

The bus wound throughout the base so the nurses could see important buildings like the base exchange, where they could buy anything from socks to underwear to shampoo to small appliances. The commissary was where groceries, paper goods, and alcoholic beverages could be purchased. Finally, Stotsenburg Station Hospital came into view, and next door were the barracks where the nurses would live while stationed there. Angelito pulled the bus up close to the front door of the barracks, and several men in US fatigues miraculously appeared to help unload the luggage.

Angelito opened the bus door, produced a dusty and tattered carpet that used to be some shade of red, and with a flourish, he stepped down out of the bus and laid the "red carpet" on the ground for the girls to walk on.

"Only the best for our American nurses," he said, "for you to walk into your new home getting the 'Red Carpet Treatment!'"

He offered a hand to each of the ladies and said "God bless you!" heartily to each nurse. When they had all stepped out of the bus, he gave each one a map of Clark Field, the hospital, and the surrounding area.

"Where did you find all these nice men to help us with our bags?" cooed one pretty nurse.

"Oh, these are the guys in mechanics where I work part of the time," Angelito replied.

"You must stay pretty busy working in two different places!" said another nurse.

"Yes, I work one-terd time in Transportation," Angelito said, holding up one finger, "and one-terd time in mechanics." He held up another finger. "And one-terd time in hospital, where you nurses will see me bring the very best medical equipment and supplies for your use in taking care of many patients." He held up another finger. "And one-terd time in the base exchange." He now had four fingers in the air.

"Wait a minute," one of the nurses said, "four thirds don't make sense! You can't work that many places!"

Angelito let out a belly laugh. "I just want to see if you are paying attention!" All the nurses and the guys unloading the luggage laughed at that.

"Hey, Angelito," shouted one of the men, "you don't do nothin' at all when you're in the mechanics department, so you can't count that one!"

Angelito feigned a heart attack and said, "How can you say that when you know I work twice as hard as you do, Freddy!"

Angelito had told the nurses that his father had died when he was very young. His mother never remarried, raising him and his sister Rosa alone. He truly believed his mother was a living angel, and he had learned to respect women and to realize what great contributions they made to society. He was looking forward to working with these new American women in Stotsenberg Hospital, which was his favorite job at Clark Field.

The nurses followed Angelito and the other men carrying all the luggage through the front door, and everyone stopped dead in their tracks. Standing inside the doorway was the head nurse, the girls' superior officer, with her hands on her hips. She did not look happy.

"Girls," she said, "this isn't a cotillion ball. It's a military installation, and I expect you to regard these quarters with the respect they are due."

She pointed up the stairs behind her. "My assistant is at the top of the stairs with your respective room assignments. Your gentlemen escorts will kindly deposit your bags here in the lobby and they will promptly take their leave. You girls may return for your bags as soon as you receive your room assignments. Supper is at 6:00 p.m. sharp in the dining room behind me, and you are expected to wear your white uniforms and caps and shoes, even in the evening. Fort Stotsenburg has been here for four decades, and it has long been a tradition in the Philippines to wear formal attire on and off base after 6:00 p.m. We are not about to change it now. Your formal attire *on base* is your same white uniforms you wear in the daytime. There will be a brief orientation following the evening meal, after which you may spend the evening in your rooms unpacking and resting up. More orientation will follow tomorrow morning, including a tour of the two-hundred-and-seventeen-bed Stotsenburg Station Hospital across the parking lot. That will be all."

With that, the head nurse saluted the girls, who saluted back. Then, she turned on her heel and marched down the hall to her office.

The nurses scurried up the steps, with a few offering a wave and mouthing "thank you" to Angelito and the startled baggage bearers.

A NICKNAME AND SOME PRETTY DRESSES

The nurses did indeed have an orientation to Stotsenburg Hospital upon their arrival. They all had experience "stateside" in military hospitals, so they knew something about taking care of soldiers and sailors of all ranks and assignments. They all agreed that, for the most part, the higher the rank—the more "spaghetti" displayed across the patients' caps and epilates—the more trouble they would give the nurses. But one of Ethel's first mornings at Stotsenburg, she went to a patient's bedside to take his vital signs, and in return she was given a very nice compliment and a new nickname.

"Well, I'll be damned," the young soldier in the first bed said to her when he saw her nametag. "I was hoping they'd give me a *nice nurse* when I came in to have my hernia repaired, but I never expected to see a *Hollywood starlet* in a starched white uniform and a nurse's cap."

"Whatever do you mean?" asked Ethel in her southern drawl. "I'm not from Hollywood. I'm from Bible Grove, Missour-a!" (Most people from the Show Me State pronounce "Missouri" as if it has an "a" on the end.)

"But your name tag says 'Miss Blaine,' and I'd swear on a stack of your Missour-a Bibles that you look *just like* the starlet Sally Blane."

Sally Blane and Ethel Blaine did look somewhat alike. Each had a heart-shaped face with wide-set, large brown eyes. Blane's hair was longer than Ethel's army regulation above-the-chin cut. Blane's lips were fuller than Ethel's, possibly a makeup artist's trick. And the starlet's eye makeup gave her a more sultry look than Ethel, who wore no enhancement to her already beautiful eyes. The two could have passed as sisters, without a doubt.

"You was in a bunch a' movies," the soldier continued. "Lemmy think... 'Silver Streak' was one movie—remember that? An' 'City Limits' an' a Charlie Chan movie, but I can't remember which one! Don't try and fool me, Sally! Your secret's safe with me." He winked at her, then he turned to the other men on the ward and shouted, "Hey, everybody! We've got us a celebrity right here in this hospital! Hollywood starlet Sally Blane is our nurse today. Say hello to her, and don't tell her I told you!"

Then he grinned at Ethel and laughed as all the boys began chanting, "Sal-LY, Sal-LY, Sal-LY!"

By now Ethel...er, Sally was turning several shades of red, but she continued checking on her patients, tending to them one by one. And each one of the patients either whistled at her or tried to hug her or kiss her, and even the sicker ones got in on the fun. One soldier in the very last bed she checked on sealed her fate.

"Well, Miss Blaine," he said, "different spelling or not, I think you just got yourself a new nickname!"

By the time Sally got back to the nurses' station that day, the women all wanted to know what was going on in Ward 3, where she had just come from.

"Oh, it's nothing," Sally said. "One patient kept insisting that I look like the movie star, Sally Blane. I told him her last name isn't even spelled the same as mine. But he wouldn't give up, and pretty soon, all the patients were calling me 'Sally,' and they said they *believed I was her.* They all said they thought I was stuck with the nickname!" Sally was almost in tears.

"Well, I think you *do* look a lot like Sally Blane," said one nurse, "whether you are related or not. And I like the nickname. I think we should all start calling you Sally!"

Within a week or two, Ethel wasn't called Ethel anymore. The nurses and the staff, as well as all the patients, began to call her Sally, and the name grew on Ethel. *"Yeah,"* she thought. *"I do like the name 'Sally' better than 'Ethel!' Besides, if they think I look like the Hollywood star named Sally, I think I'll keep it."*

COLLABORATIVE DATING ARMY STYLE

Idyllic days and warm, breezy nights embraced the nurses as well as the many (hopefully single) men they saw every day in their common roles of caring for others and living in adjacent barracks. To say that love—or something a whole lot like it—was in the air was an understatement. The atmosphere was literally pulsating with the attraction between the sexes. The nurses had blonde, brunette, red, dark brown, and black hair, and every shade in between, subject to a chemical change in color once in a while. They were fair-complected or freckle-faced or suntanned or ruddy. Their figures were ample or slender or somewhere in between. They were quiet and shy, bubbly and sociable, and outgoing and full of surprises. And there were men who preferred each of these types of women and men who liked them all. The pairings were inevitable, and the pleasant climate made an enticing environment for getting together.

Although the nurses didn't talk about the invitations they were getting from the men on base in front of their head nurse, there was a lot of chatter after the girls retired for the night. Some had already accepted dates at the first opportunity, and several had brought lovely evening gowns from home. They modeled their gowns for each other, and those who had more than one graciously loaned their spare gowns to the others.

"Don't let me see you and Captain Harvey at the Jai Ali!" teased one redheaded nurse. "That's where my date and I are going, and I might want to wear the dress I'm loaning you another night!"

"Hey, does somebody have an eye shadow that would match this dress?" another nurse, who was painfully shy, asked.

"I have a necklace that would go perfectly with the dress you're going to wear. Let me go find it in my room!"

Sally stayed very quiet while the other nurses were talking about their dates. Sally had been asked out a few times, but she said "no" every time. She knew people dressed in their finest clothes in the evening in the Philippines. But she didn't have any dresses like the other women brought from home. Nobody in Bible Grove, Missouri, ever dressed like that, and clothing for dates when she was in nursing school in San Diego was much less formal. Sally didn't expect she could accept any dates at all now, at least not until she could save enough money to buy even one of these fabulous dresses the other girls had.

One popular nurse noticed that Sally wasn't getting in on the fun of planning their dates. She walked down the hall to where Sally was standing in the doorway of her room, watching but not participating in the banter between the girls.

"What's wrong, Sally?" the nurse asked her. "Didn't you bring any gowns to wear out in the clubs here?"

"No, I didn't bring any, and I can't afford to buy any!" Sally replied.

"Well, we need to take you down to Olongapo's Clothing Store. You'll find plenty there, and the Tagalog owner is a terrific tailor, so he can alter anything or sew something for you for a fraction of what you'd pay stateside."

"Really?" Sally said. "Do the dresses look cheap?"

"Come look," the nurse said. I have two a friend here bought for me in my closet."

Sally padded down the hall in her house slippers to the girl's room.

"Oh my goodness!" Sally picked up the first dress and said, "It's beautiful!"

"How much do you think I paid for that dress?"

Sally thought for a moment. "Well, the most I ever paid for a dress back home—and it was just a regular old church dress—was about five dollars."

The other nurse scoffed. "Here in the Philippines, you can buy a beautiful evening dress like these for about $3 American, and Olangapos *will take American cash!*"

"Well, what are we waiting for?" Sally cried. "Will you take me to this Olan...Oling..."

"Olongapos! The next day we have off together, we'll take the train into Manila and get you fixed up. He'll even let you pay for the dresses on time."

And so, the very next time the two nurses had a day off together, Sally went with her friend to the tailor named Olongapos.

Olongapos Fine Dresses and Menswear was an institution in Manila. All the high-class ladies and gentlemen shopped there for evening wear, including US military personnel and their spouses, as well as "ex-pats," people from another country who made their permanent residence in the Philippines. Ex-patriots from other nations exuded a certain mystique, and the nurses were wary of them. Foreign-born residents, including Americans, might not always be trustworthy in relaying details about their former lives. But most of the nurses found other suitors. They had their eyes on the American officers and the physicians and other health personnel at Stotsenburg and the other military hospitals in the area. Those men were required to wear their "dress white" uniforms after 6:00 p.m., so it was easy to tell the difference between them and the ex-pats.

When Sally and several other nurses took the train to Manila to look for dresses, Felix Olongapos welcomed them, quite literally, with open arms. When she saw what looked like a fairytale candy land of beautiful dresses of every design and every fabric and every color of the rainbow, Sally's jaw just dropped.

"Sally, close your mouth!" whispered the tall, slender nurse who had suggested they go to the dress shop.

"What?! Oh, sorry!" Sally shut her mouth but could not keep it shut when she saw the beautiful styles and fabrics.

"You're doing it again!" whispered her companion. "Let's have you try on some dresses and change your expression to a smile!"

After trying on what seemed like a couple hundred dresses, Sally finally settled on a lavender eyelet form-fitting floor-length gown with short puffy sleeves, and her favorite of all the dresses she tried on, a pink and green plaid satin sundress with a flared skirt that she thought looked like something a girl would sew for her hometown county fair fashion contest. Each dress cost about $3.00 American money, and Sally ordered two more dresses to be custom-made and ready in one week.

While the girls were riding the train back to Clark Field, a discussion ensued about why each of the nurses had asked to come to the Philippines.

"I thought it sounded like paradise!" said one girl from North Dakota.

"You were right about that," said another one from Ohio. "It *is* paradise!"

Another girl from Los Angeles said she was interested in seeing as much of the world as possible while in the service, and the Philippines sounded like a great start.

"When I was in fifth grade," Sally said, "we had a geography lesson about Southeast Asia, and I guess I said to my teacher, 'I'm going to the Philippines when I grow up!' I don't remember saying it, but they told me I did. We learned that the Philippines is a US Territory until 1946, and it's 1941 now. I wanted to go while the US was still in charge because it felt safer."

"I didn't know it's a US territory!" said another nurse. "I guess we *should* feel pretty safe!"

"That's what I think," said Sally. "With the United States in control, this must be one of the safest places anywhere. It's good to be here!"

And all the nurses agreed.

AXIS OF POWER

And the Abyss began hissing again. The evil within the jaws of the Abyss was getting restless for action. There were terrible things on the horizon that none of these new nurses could even imagine. Nor could the rest of the world fathom what three dictators' regimes were planning together—Hitler in Germany, Mussolini in Italy, and Hirohito's war-hungry generals in Japan—so they could take over the world. The "Axis of Power" believed they would prevail.

BUILDING UP TO SOMETHING

The summer of 1941 went by in a flash. The dresses the nurses bought in Manila were put to good use as each of them accepted invitation after invitation to accompany handsome young servicemen to night clubs and concerts in Manila. As they dressed for their evening dates, the chatter was exuberant.

"Oh, Sally! That gingham green sundress is just about the sweetest dress I've seen in ages! It is *perfect* on you!"

"Thank you! I like it too!"

Sally liked the dress, and she liked all the attention she was getting from a number of men in the hospitals and at the base exchange (a retail store on a military base where service members could purchase a variety of goods, including clothing, personal items, and household supplies) and the commissary (a grocery store on a military base where service members could buy food and other household necessities).

By mid-September 1841, Sally had invitations from men to attend everything from dining and dancing to the opera and ballet to picnics and road trips around the island of Luzon, on which Clark Air Base and Manila both sat. There was dancing on outdoor terraces amid fragrant blossoms beneath moonlit skies. There were bottomless cocktails with exotic titles served up in sparkling fancy glasses or hollowed-out pineapple and coconut shells. The local cuisine included ocean fish and seafood caught the same day they were prepared, and over-the-top desserts like flaming Bananas Foster and Coconut Mango Bread Pudding with Rum Sauce. The entertainment in Manila rivaled anything offered in any other well-known metropolis in the world. In fact, Manila was dubbed the Havana of the Pacific. The decadence was enough to make a young woman's head spin. Enjoying that decadence with a handsome man in an all-white dress uniform took the experience to a whole new level.

The climate in the Philippines is tropical and maritime, with warm temperatures and high humidity, coupled with abundant rainfall. On Luzon, it was not uncommon to have 150 inches of rain a year. This dampened many evenings of dancing under the stars, but there were plenty of indoor opportunities to enjoy. Gambling, legal and illegal, has been available in the Philippine archipelago since the sixteen hundreds, and the US military personnel spent many hours supporting the gambling establishments. Manila also offered a full array of indoor cultural events, including concerts, operas, and plays. Entertainment was available in Manila rain or shine.

It wasn't long until the nurses began to talk among themselves about Christmas and all the opportunities to wear new and different dresses to the festivities planned in Manila and right on the army base. The officers club would of course have its own gala, and every club and venue in Manila was poised to offer the best and most memorable holiday experience. Movie theaters were showing "Ball of Fire" with Barbara Stanwyck and Gary Cooper, and "Mr. Smith Goes To Washington," starring Jimmy Stewart.

Back at Clark Field and Stotsenburg Hospital, Sally noticed a difference in the men who were coming to serve there. For one thing, they were greater in number, and for another, they didn't seem to have their dress white uniforms with them. Was it possible they were coming in as part of a troop buildup, and not to escort pretty nurses to fancy balls and renowned concerts and plays? The international news told of increasing military presence in other places in the world, like the United Kingdom, North Africa, and the South Pacific (on the doorstep of the Philippines). One would have to be blind not to see the "rumors of wars" in other parts of the world. But nothing had been said and no training held about what to do if war came close to the Americans in the Philippines.

One night at dinnertime in the hospital staff dining room, Sally and some other nurses were invited to sit at the table with the chief nurse and other higher-ranking officers.

Sally leaned over and quietly asked the chief nurse, "Don't you think it would be a good idea for us to get some heavy clothing organized and ready to wear in case we had to move into Manila and had to bivouac on the way down?"

The chief nurse was from Canada and Sally believed the Canadians might be willing to talk about troop buildup more freely than their tight-lipped American counter-parts.

Her superior officer looked Sally square in the face and said, "I shall do no such thing…unless and until we receive orders from headquarters!" And with that, all talk about the potential for war was immediately stopped.

Little did the young nurses know that the "orders from headquarters" would definitely come, sooner rather than later. But the "orders" would come from the Japanese "headquarters."

PROCUREMENTS

The door of the freight elevator on Ward 3 at Stotsenburg Hospital opened and a large utility cart overfilled with medical supplies came out with no one pushing it. Or at least it appeared no one was pushing it until the cart stopped at the nurses' station and Angelito stepped out from behind his giant pile of what he called "procurements." Sally was writing in a patient chart when he spotted her.

"Miss Sally Blaine! I heard all about your name change." He moved around her slowly, taking in all sides of her except the front, which was facing the counter where she had been writing. "I like the nickname. It suits you perfectly!"

Sally eyed him warily. "You like it, huh? I kinda do too but everybody makes fun of me now, saying I must really be the movie star." She sighed. "The joke is getting *a little old.*"

Angelito smiled and pointed to his cart.

"See? I bring you tip-top medical equipment for your procurement."

"You mean for us to use?"

"Yes, yes, of course! I bring you most special and necessary medical items for your use. Tell me now what things you exactly need, and I will give you. If I don't have, I will find. Is *huge* hospital"—he stretched his arms out wide—"and we have everything for you and your patients and your doctors. Please, now tell me what you need."

Sally thought for a moment. "Well, our rolled bandage supply was getting low last time I was in the supply room. And bedpans seem to go missing frequently around here…"

"Bandages I have, I will give you plenty. But the bedpans, they are a problem. The enlisted men think it is funny to drink beer out of them—after they wash good, of course!"

Sally and the other nurses behind the desk made faces.

"That's disgusting!" said one.

"Whatever happened to drinking beer from a plain old glass? Or the bottle!" said another.

"Yes, yes, I know. It seems really—how you say? 'Harm your stomach?'"

"Nauseating!" the nurses cried in unison.

"But last time I looked, they had some of the bedpans in the Surgical Department where they don't need. I will try to get them for you."

"Why on earth are they keeping so many down there? Their patients are *asleep!*"

"I'll bet they use them for their morning coffee," Sally said.

"EWE!" came the combined response.

"Okay, okay," Angelito interrupted. "Here are the rolled bandages and I go work on procurement for the bedpans. You ladies have a blessed day and remember God has brought you to this beautiful island that He made for us all to enjoy. Say your prayers and ask God to be with you at all times, even when you go dancing with the men friends."

"How do you know about *that?*" one of the nurses asked.

"Is *small* hospital when stories come around." He gave them a mischievous grin.

"Thanks, Angelito, we really appreciate it when you bring us supplies," Sally said as she went back to writing in her patients' charts. *Angelito is so nice,* Sally thought. *No matter what he's doing, he works hard at it, and he is always pleasant to talk to. Plus, he is so dedicated to his mother and to his God.*

The nurses would continue to see Angelito in his many roles at Clark Field. If he was driving a delivery truck on base, on his way to fulfill an order or pick up something to be hauled to someplace else, he would wave at the nurses as they walked to and from their barracks. He appeared numerous times a week with one of the chaplains, and together they delivered communion to the patients as well as the hospital staff and even the commanding officers who asked for it. Angelito would show up at the hospital at seemingly any hour, as if he never slept or ate or went home. Some rumors started that Angelito was kind of a spy for the commanding officers of Clark, but some said no, he's not even real. He's actually an angel. No one can be so cheerful all the time, night or day, and the way he speaks about his faith, well, where are his wings? He can't be real! He must be some kind of spirit-being who has come to minister to the staff and the patients and everyone at Clark. Still others said he was just an ordinary young man who hasn't gotten up the courage to ask one of the nurses out on a date. But all agreed, Angelito was a special kind of friend to everyone he met, and most especially to the nurses.

Rumor had it that Angelito had lied about his age to join the Philippine Militia, which had a minimum age of sixteen to join. He did look young, maybe fourteen or fifteen, but no one could believe he would *lie*! After all, he could not be both an angel *and* a liar!

PART III

RULES OF ENGAGEMENT

"Why were the generals so insistent that we engage in this war? I do not believe it is right, but they keep telling me this is a golden opportunity that cannot be allowed to pass by! I try talking to them, but they insult me with their "knowledge and experience." They treat me like a child, as if I don't know right from wrong. How dare they say these things behind my back? I hear from others what is being said. But Japanese emperors are divine, and they know *that*. I do not wish to be forced into agreeing with something I do not believe in nor stand for. I know what is right: we should not be persuaded to enter this unholy allegiance with the others who believe they will rule the world. Mussolini and Hitler think they are some sort of gods, but they are not like our Japanese rulers. Japan should have normal relations with other nations and not bludgeon other societies into oblivion because we think we are stronger! And if we don't prevail in this horrid war they are proposing, what happens then? Do we lose our way of life and suffer untold death and destruction in our own land? What then have we proven? Nothing! The French philosopher Voltaire said, 'To the living we owe *respect but to the dead we owe only the truth.' I will meet with these war mongers and tell them I do not approve of this aggression toward other nations, I will make them understand!"*

Hirohito paced the floor as his thoughts consumed him.

But Prime Minister Hideki Tojo and the stubborn generals bullied the young emperor to the point where he turned a blind eye to their plans to bomb Pearl Harbor, Clark Field, and many other targets. The genie was out of the bottle now, and there was simply no way to put it back inside. He eventually would be worn down by the war mongers and he would agree with their plans. This time the Abyss did not hiss.

The Abyss growled.

THE OTHER PEARL HARBOR

The Japanese invasion of the Philippines began on December 8th, 1941, just ten hours after the attack on Pearl Harbor. The initial landings took place on a small island about 450 miles south of Manila.

Also bombed that day were Camp John Hay (about sixty miles north of Clark Army Air Base, where Sally was stationed), Clark Air Base (where Sally was, stationed), and Naval Station Sangley Point (only eight miles from Manila). These bombings and subsequent battles marked the beginning of the Japanese occupation of the Philippines, which lasted until 1945.

On December 10th, Japanese forces landed on a small island off the northern coast of Luzon, and on the 12th, they secured key positions in the southern part of Luzon. Also by December 12, the American Asiatic Fleet had withdrawn from the Philippines to Java due to the overwhelming Japanese attacks.

By December 22nd, the Imperial Japanese Army had launched a major attack at the Lingayen Gulf on Luzon, beginning their advance toward Manila. Japanese General Masaharu Homa landed in the Lingayen Gulf, which proved to be an important place to engage with a poorly *equipped contingency of American and Filipino troops. With only a minor skirmish, the Japanese were able to invade and occupy the Gulf. The day of that defeat, American General Douglas MacArthur issued the order for US hospitals to evacuate all staff and patients and to retreat to the jungles of the Bataan Peninsula.*

THIS IS IT, ISN'T IT?

Sally and some of her nurse friends were gone the whole weekend of December 6th to the 8th. A group of them had ridden the train to Manila from Stotsenberg Hospital. The girls rented a hotel room, ate their meals out, and went to some of the well-known dance clubs on Friday and Saturday evenings. You might say they painted the town red, but they paid the price riding the train back north to Clark Air Base overnight. They arrived back at the barracks at about 6:00 a.m. Some of the nurses went right to the hospital to work the early shift, but Sally didn't have to work until the next day. After she got back to her room in the women's barracks, she was asleep before she hit the pillow. Soon, an older nurse named Wila, who outranked Sally, began shaking her.

"Wake up!" said Wila. "Pearl Harbor's been bombed!"

Well, Sally thought that sounded bad, but in her tired brain, she reasoned that Pearl Harbor was a long way away, so that didn't affect the Americans stationed in Manila. And anyway, Wila didn't say *who* bombed Pearl Harbor. Sally expected it was the Japanese, but she didn't think about the fact that the Philippines was a lot closer to Japan than Hawaii.

Wila was having none of this nonsense. She came back shortly and almost tore Sally's mosquito net off her bed.

"You get up right now," she said to Sally. "Get up out of that bed, because Camp John Hay has been bombed now."

Now that was only a little over sixty miles north of Clark Field and Stotsenberg Hospital, so that got Sally's attention. She got up and got dressed, and everyone who wasn't at the hospital went down to eat lunch.

And nothing happened. It was so quiet, no one knew what to make of the situation. When the news came that John Hay had been bombed, some of the Clark Field pilots jumped in their planes and took off to go see what was happening at the northern facility. They came back quickly because whoever was doing the bombing had now disappeared. And it was true, no one was certain at first exactly who had bombed the camp on the Philippines's biggest island, Luzon.

The next day, still no sight of the planes doing the bombing. Sally was to go to work at 3:00 that day, so after lunch, she went upstairs to put on her nurse's uniform. She put her foot up on a footstool to tie her shoelace, and she felt a kind of shudder that made her heart pound. Even the barracks building shook a bit. She turned to look out the window and saw a huge flash of light, past the hospital where the planes were lined up in neat little rows. Except there were no more planes, just twisted metal and shattered glass, which didn't make sense because the planes were there only moments ago! Then she heard a deafening noise that made her block her ears. Her heart rate sped up. Instantly there was black smoke. Billows and billows of black smoke. The air raid sirens screamed in protest. Sally knew instinctively what this meant: the war had finally come to their very doorstep.

She slowly walked to the top of the stairs, as if in a bad dream. She could feel her heart racing and she could already smell the acrid odor of all that black smoke. Her chief nurse was at the bottom of the stairs looking up at Sally. Other nurses had begun to gather around their superior to hear orders of what to do next. Sally had a fleeting thought about the Canadian chief nurse telling her not to be talking about an escape plan. Wasn't that just a few days ago? And now, here they were, unprepared for what was to come.

Sally spoke to the chief nurse from the top of the stairs. "This is it, isn't it?"

The chief nurse looked up at Sally and said, "I suppose it is." Then the chief nurse walked away.

As if in slow motion, Sally thought about what she needed to grab before heading for the hospital. Her cosmetic bag. That was all that crossed her mind. *I just have to have my lipstick and my comb and my powder with me. That's all that matters right now.* She ran back to her room and grabbed the little zippered bag with the dogwood flower print that said *Scotland County Fair* on it. She had admired it one Saturday night when she went to the fair with a classmate. He won it for her in a carnival game that night, and Sally had used it ever since.

Sally didn't enjoy the euphoric feeling very long. Soon she was running to the hospital as fast as her trembling legs would carry her. Her hair was flying, her lungs were burning, her feet slammed against the hard asphalt parking lot. She thought her heart would burst. She finally got to her station and...*nothing happened.* It was all so quiet, and everyone—nurses, doctors, technicians, housekeepers—stood quietly waiting for whatever was going to happen next.

Then the Japanese planes returned and began strafing the parking lot between the hospital and the barracks. A few nurses were still coming across the tarmac from the barracks, and they began running for their lives. Sally watched out a hospital window, holding her breath to see the young women in such danger. But they all made it to the hospital, and the word got around that all the nurses and all the doctors were accounted for. And every one of them was needed.

About fifteen minutes after the strafing stopped and the Japanese planes left again, the screaming sirens from the ambulances could be heard coming from the direction of Clark Field, adjacent to the hospital grounds. So many casualties were being unloaded at the ER door—two, sometimes three or four to an ambulance. The rapid trauma assessments were being shouted out by the arriving ambulance drivers so quickly that it was hard to tell which patients had which type of traumatic wounds. The screams of the injured rose among the shouts of staff, creating a cacophony of human voices.

Sally didn't recognize any of the medical team except the chaplain, and she watched him come in with casualties and go right back out in another ambulance. Sally had met the chaplain and got to know him. She sat with him at meals and played an occasional board game with him and others. But she had never seen him in any kind of crisis, and she was impressed by how much medical knowledge he was relaying right along with the ambulance drivers. He sounded like he'd spent a lot of time in war zones.

About the fourth or fifth trip, Sally saw the chaplain come in on an ambulance; she was tending to a patient who had been blown off his feet by the initial bomb and had landed on his head. The patient had to have stitches in the head wound, and Sally was preparing to bandage him up. She saw the chaplain heading straight for where she was working.

"Sally," the chaplain called out, "there's a young Filipino boy asking for you. He just came in on Ambulance 14."

"Asking for *me?*" Sally asked. "I don't know who that would..."

"Says to tell you his name is Angelito."

"Angelito? Oh, NO!"

Sally's heart was pounding. She was used to seeing her colleagues and other medical personnel sick or slightly injured, but the casualties that were coming in now were severe: gaping chest wounds that would not stop bleeding, head injuries that left men unconscious, and extremity wounds including severely injured hands and feet, as well as traumatic injuries and broken bones in legs and arms. There were also pneumothoraces (punctured and collapsed lungs) and other serious internal injuries and bleeding. Her mind was racing. What wounds would she find Angelito had sustained?

She ran to the entrance of the ER. Sure enough, Angelito was lying on a gurney with another nurse attending him and a doctor beginning an assessment.

"Please let me through," Sally said. "I know this young man!"

Angelito tried to sit up on the gurney, but he grabbed his right leg and screamed in pain.

"Where is my rosary?" Angelito cried. "Miss Sally! Are you here? I am hurt! Those dirty rotten…"

"I'm right here, Angelito! Where are you hurt?"

The doctor answered. "He has a pretty deep leg wound but no apparent broken bones. We'll take him to X-ray to make sure nothing's broken. He was lucky. Some of these strafing victims have internal injuries. This one should be up and around in no time."

"Oh, thank God, Angelito! Did you hear the doctor? You will be okay!"

"I must be okay," said Angelito. "I must take care of you, Miss Sally, and all the other nice American nurses! I must do procurements for you and drive the bus with the red carpet and help you carry things. And I must pray for you, that you and all the wonderful nurses at Stotsenberg Hospital will know how much God loves each one of you! God sings over each of you every day, and he protects you in the safety of his wings. You are HEROES!"

"Oh, Angelito!" said Sally. "We are NOT heroes! We are just doing our job, like we did stateside before we came to the Philippines!"

"You are MORE than heroes," Angelito said. "God will bless each of you and you will see how He works in all of us for the good of the Kingdom. God has anointed each of you to do His healing here on earth. I will be better soon.

God is so good to me!" He pulled a rosary out of his pants pocket and raised the crucifix hanging around his neck to his lips.

A Catholic chaplain approached the gurney Angelito lay on.

"What's all this fuss," the chaplain said. "Angelito, what's going on?"

Sally turned to the chaplain. "You know this young man?"

"Everybody knows Angelito," the chaplain said. "He is one of Christ's true ambassadors on earth. He helps me give communion to the patients as well as the staff whenever he's not working around here in some other capacity!"

Sally heard her name being called from across the ER. She turned and saw that there were many more soldiers being brought in from the sites of the bombings. Many were injured severely. Some were clearly in a lot of pain and were groaning for someone to help them. The burn cases were the worst; their screams were enough to take Sally's breath away.

"Nurse Blaine! You're needed over here!"

"Angelito, I have to go! You do what the doctor says, and he will take good care of you!"

"God be with you, Miss Sally, and God will be with the doctor who is helping me."

Sally squeezed Angelito's shoulder, nodded at the chaplain, and sprinted to where the ever-growing number of patients were being brought into the emergency room. After Clark Field was bombed and the casualties began pouring in, Sally and the other nurses learned quickly what it meant to be responding to war injuries. The medical "school of hard knocks" begins and ends with war casualties.

TRIAGE

The word "triage" is derived from the French term, trier, meaning "to sort." The word was initially used for sorting food products. Its first known medical use was in World War I when the French used it to apply to the sorting of casualties. Sally and the medical staff at Philippine-based military hospitals used the term for the process of deciding which patients would be treated first. This was a difficult job and did not always mean the most critically wounded soldiers were attended to first.

Often, the emergency care doctors and surgeons in war hospitals had to make the tough call not to treat a patient who clearly was close to death and could not be helped fast enough or because the hospital lacked the equipment and/or supplies to treat the most severe injuries. A nurse and one or more chaplains were assigned to the area where these patients were staged, with their only job being to keep the patients comfortable until their lives ended. Sally and the other nurses rotated in and out of this duty, and they all found it to be one of the hardest assignments. It's a dismal piece of the fabric of any hospital, never more so than in a war zone. It is a particularly important place in a combat hospital because of the high number of dead and dying patients there.

Some patients succumbed to their injuries quickly, but for others, the dying could take hours or days. The nurses all were uncomfortable with a shift change moving them out of this area, which came to be known as the "dead house." It was often nearly impossible to tell these patients that the person who had been caring for them for a whole eight- or twelve-hour shift now had to pass these catastrophically injured patients off to another nurse. But the nurses trusted each other that the staff on the next shift would grant the patient the same heartfelt care going forward.

The emergency rush lasted all day. Every single bed in Stotsenberg Hospital was needed for the trauma patients coming in. Perhaps a hundred casualties were brought to the ER that day, and the hospital barely had enough beds for them with the current occupancy already stretched to the max. Anyone capable of being treated as an outpatient was asked to leave. There was a lull in the airstrikes, but then the real attacks began.

LEAVING CLARK

The first time Clark Field was bombed by the Japanese, everyone on duty knew the plan. At the hospital, the patients were to be moved to the basement of the building, where they had the best chance of not being injured in the bombing. Several storage rooms had been cleared of furniture, scrubbed clean, and made ready for the patients. The bombs kept falling, but not one hit the hospital. The Japanese kept up a continuous barrage every day for almost three weeks. And each time, everyone had to take cover. This lasted from December 8th until the 24th, Christmas Eve. During this time, Sally and a new nurse named Ann were finally off duty for a couple of days. Ann had been moved from another hospital to help out. The two girls decided to go swimming, and both being Midwest girls, they thought donning their bathing suits in December was crazy. They had a grand time. It was good they didn't get caught because the head nurse would not have thought it was cute at all. The girls were lucky to get back to the barracks undetected.

The next day, things began to change rapidly. The bombs were getting closer and closer to the hospital, and the powers that be decided the patients and the medical staff had to be evacuated. The patients were loaded onto trains, and the medical staff came on board to make sure IVs were still inserted and bandages had not slipped. A small number of doctors and nurses stayed on the train and rode with the patients to Manila. The others were getting ready to board a bus when the air raid siren went off. They all had to take cover, and there was a great scramble to get someplace safe.

Sally saw a culvert and thought that was a terrific place to take cover. She crawled into a drainage pipe so small, she could not use her arms to move forward; she had to shimmy in. She took a deep breath and started into the culvert. It was then she realized there was an iguana not much smaller than her staring directly at her. She tried to shimmy right back out of the culvert, but she was wearing riding boots, and one got stuck. The iguana did not look happy. Sally couldn't move. It was a wartime standoff between woman and lizard. Sally shimmied harder and finally got her foot unstuck. She nearly bolted out of the culvert and came face to face with the Filipino cook from the nurses' barracks.

"Oh, Missy Blaine, Missy Blaine, Missy Blaine!" he said, wringing his hands. "I want to help you but I could not do so!"

"I'm okay now," Sally said, "and the bombs seem to have quit for the moment. Let's make a run for the buses."

A CUP OF CHRISTMAS FEAR

No one was surprised to see that Angelito had managed to get assigned to drive the bus transporting the nurses to the bigger hospital in Manila. He was a young man with many surprising talents, including getting assignments to work with the nurses. He greeted them with his usual positive attitude. Only a few days had passed since he had been injured during the bombing of Clark Field, but Sally knew Angelito was determined to keep his passengers in the spirit of the Christmas season.

"Hellooooooooo, Ladies!" he squeaked into the microphone. "We are evacuating the patients, yes? And I know God will be with us in this blessed season of the birth of our Lord Jesus Christ. We will celebrate the season tonight, yes? I have for you sheets of American Christmas carols, and we sing them together, yes?" He began passing out sheets of song lyrics, making sure each nurse took one as he walked the aisle to the back of the bus.

Angelito started the bus and it lurched into gear to join the parade of ambulances, supply trucks, and other military vehicles headed into Manila. The patients had already been loaded on train cars with attending medical staff to keep them safe and comfortable.

"But, Angelito," one nurse called out, "no one is here to accompany us! There are no instruments on the bus that I can see."

"Ah, have faith, please, Miss Nurse! I have been practicing in my spare time and I will sing with you while I drive you. I will have this microphone on in the front." He grinned as he pulled the mic down in front of himself. "We start with 'O Little Town of Bethlehem,' first tune."

And with that he began to sing in a rich tenor voice so compelling that the nurses soon all joined in. After each song, Angelito went back over the lyrics, pointing out what a wonderful God it was who came to live with ordinary people and to teach his ways to them. A few of the nurses rolled their eyes and snickered to each other. But most of them appreciated Angelito's positive attitude and his efforts to help everyone remember what the season of Christmas was about.

As they drove through the gates of the beleaguered Clark Field, many signs pointed toward a wartime atmosphere. The gates were heavily guarded now by military police with big guns. A banner across the gate still wished those entering a "Merry Christmas and Happy New Year," but every nurse on the bus wondered in what state the Philippine Islands would be by Christmas. The sacred day was less than two weeks away, and some nurses had brought bags of wrapped gifts with them. Sally wondered if they would ever see anyone opening them.

After "Oh Little Town of Bethlehem," they sang "Hark the Herald Angels Sing" while passing through the quiet countryside, followed by "Joy to the World" as they rode through a small town. The civilian community looked perfectly normal. Holiday decorations were everywhere. The people were going about their lives and getting ready for Christmas celebrations as if the American military installations had never been bombed. It seemed the people didn't know the island nation had been invaded, or perhaps they thought the American troops had beaten back the Japanese forces. Or they were just holding their breath until they couldn't deny what was happening anymore.

Next was a familiar song, and Sally knew most of the words.

God rest ye merry gentlemen/Let nothing you dismay/For Jesus Christ our Savior/Was born on Christmas Day/To save us all from Satan's pow'r…

Suddenly she stopped singing. Those words, *Save us all from Satan's pow'r…* Sally felt a darkness descending over her. As much as she appreciated Angelito's efforts to keep the nurses' spirits high, Sally knew the signs were all around them: the Japanese *had* invaded the country, they *had* destroyed a great many US aircraft and buildings, and now they *had* forced the hospital to close. She thought of Stotsenberg Hospital and what might become of that building. The nurses had left most of their belongings in the barracks, all Sally's pretty dresses and jewelry for each outfit. She managed to pack some of her belongings—including her precious cosmetic kit—in a duffel bag. But things she had collected since her arrival here were mostly gone now. She knew instinctively they would never return to retrieve them. They were only told to bring their starched white nurses' uniforms, white nylon stockings and white shoes, and of course, their nurses' white hats.

Sally shuddered at their situation. *To save us all from Satan's power?* Satan seemed alive and determined to make life very, very difficult. Difficult indeed.

AN UNSETTLING QUIET

The Abyss didn't hiss. It didn't growl. It just cast a dark net of fear over the bus full of nurses. They thought the roaring in their ears was odd. They didn't suspect that Pure Evil was coming for each one of them.

WHAT'S THE BIG IDEA?

As the bus pulled into the outskirts of Manila, the nurses could clearly see it wasn't much safer than Clark Field. They were coming to Sternberg Hospital, another American military facility with a name similar to the one they left. But by the time they arrived, they only saw staff moving patients and equipment *out* of the hospital.

"What's the big idea?" one nurse cried out her open window. "We are nurses coming in from Stotsenberg after we were bombed, to work in *this* hospital! Patients came earlier by train. Why are you moving out?"

"It's not safe here either," a man replied. "You might as well follow us to a new site!"

The man explained that the hospitals were "sitting targets" for the Japanese, who were bombing all kinds of targets, both military and civilian. The hospital administrators had decided the patients would be secretly disbursed to a variety of smaller makeshift "emergency annexes" for the time being. He had no idea where these nurses would be sent.

"Well, what's happened to our patients who came here ahead of us by train?" another nurse asked.

"I don't know for sure, but they didn't unload them here, I can tell you that!" the man hollered.

Angelito spoke up now. "We'll just turn the bus around and follow these guys wherever they are going!"

As they joined the long caravan of every imaginable military vehicle, Sally sat back in her seat and tried to relax. She was developing a headache, and she knew she could not afford to be compromised in any way. Events were unfolding rapidly, and things did not look good. Sally thought she heard the same roaring in her ears she had heard the first day she arrived in Manila, when the bus full of nurses drove past the Santo Tomas University. She shook her head and told herself the roaring sound had to be the many vehicles in the convoy.

The Abyss hissed underneath the highway along which the column of vehicles drove. Danger was everywhere, but the nurses didn't know how bad things would become.

It was soon clear that even Manila was too dangerous for the patients and their caregivers. Things were moving so fast. It was hard to know from minute-to-minute what orders were coming next. Sally thought wistfully about her suggestion to her commanding officer at dinner just a week ago that perhaps they would be wise to pull together some warm clothes and other provisions in case they needed to flee the Japanese quickly. Sally was rebuffed. She felt hurt and angry now. Had the officer been holding back the truth? Or had she herself missed the clues, the truth that was now so clear to them all?

And yet, here they were, their bus following the ever-growing caravan of military personnel moving toward the entrance to the foreboding jungle of the Bataan Peninsula.

PART IV

WAR PLAN ORANGE-3

In July 1941, a few months before the outbreak of the Pacific War between the United States and the Empire of Japan, Lt. General Douglas MacArthur was recalled from retirement to active duty with the United States. He became the commander of United States Army Forces in the Far East (USAFFE), uniting the Philippine and United States Armies under one command. Later, during World War II, on April 18, 1942, MacArthur became Supreme Commander, Southwest Pacific Area (SWPA), covering the Philippines, Australia, the Netherlands East Indies, and New Guinea. MacArthur played a crucial role in the defense of the Philippines.

Plans for the Philippines defense had been in existence for many years before World War II. The latest revision of these plans, completed in April 1941 (seven months before Pearl Harbor and the invasion of the Philippines by Japanese forces), was called War Plan Orange-3 (WPO-3). This was one of the many "color" plans developed during the prewar years. Each color plan dealt with a different situation, ORANGE covering an emergency in which only the United States and Japan would be involved. The plan was politically unrealistic and *completely outdated by the end of 1941. Tactically, however, the plan was an excellent one and its provisions for defense were applicable under any local situation.*

Under WPO-3, American troops were not to fight anywhere but in Central Luzon, the largest of the Philippine Islands on which Manila is situated. The mission was to hold the entrance to Manila Bay with US Naval ships and deny its use to Japanese nautical forces. U.S. Army troops were to prevent enemy landings. If this effort failed, they were to defeat any Japanese forces that succeeded in landing. If, despite these attempts, the enemy proved successful, the troops were to engage in delaying action while also ensuring the defense of Manila Bay. The Americans were to make every attempt to hold back the Japanese advance while withdrawing to the Bataan Peninsula. Bataan, recognized as the key to the control of Manila Bay, was to be defended to the "last extremity." Lack of funding for this effort became a major issue from the outset of the war with Japan.

When it was clear that the Manila corridor, from Clark Field in the north to southern Luzon Medical Center in the south, was under siege by the Japanese, the decision was made to move the entire medical staff and all patients who had been cared for in military hospitals to the relative safety of the jungles on the Bataan Peninsula. This mass relocation of medical staff, patients, supply workers, and many other employees began on Christmas Eve 1941.

JUNGLE HOSPITALS

The Bataan Peninsula is covered by dense forests of mahogany, teak, and mangrove, which give way to grasslands and stands of bamboo and rattan nearing the coasts. The bulldozers came first. They cleared the way for the jungle hospitals to be set up.

A steep mountain range cuts through the area, with 4,200-foot-high Mount Natib to the north. The American and Filipino troops set up an infantry line from Bagac on the west coast to Orion on the east as soon as it became apparent where the Japanese Imperial Army would launch their ground attack. The first patients, most of whom had been housed in the military hospitals along the length of Luzon Island, came almost before the doctors and nurses charged with treating them were there themselves, within hours of the area being cleared for the field hospitals.

The mosquitos had already set up shop, so when the first humans came on the scene, the disease-carrying insects went to work. It would be safe to say the first cases of malaria were well underway before the humans had been encamped there for one day. When an infected female Anopheles mosquito bites a person, a parasite gets *passed to the human's bloodstream. The parasite travels to the liver, where it multiplies before infecting red blood cells, leading to fever, chills, sweating, headaches, muscle aches, nausea, and debilitating fatigue. For treatment of malaria, the Bataan medical staff relied on quinine, an antimalarial drug derived from the bark of the cinchona tree. Because supplies were quickly in short supply, many medical staff, active-duty soldiers, and patients suffered from untreated malaria. The resilience of the troops in such harsh environments is a testament to their determination.*

Mount Bataan, 4,700 feet high, stood sentinel in the south of the peninsula, about seventy miles north of Corregidor Island. The dense forests and steep slopes of Mount Bataan and Mount Natib provided natural cover and made it challenging for the Japanese forces to advance, forming a bowl in the middle of the peninsula, where the American and Filipino Armies set up their field hospitals.

Seven-inch-tall tarsiers, one of the world's smallest primates, are among the wildlife found on the peninsula. The tiny monkeys' adorable huge eyes study their surroundings for danger. Measuring 3 ½ to 6 inches plus a tail sometimes twice that length, these tiny leaping monkeys are harmless but annoying when they become curious. When nearby humans who are, say, performing a delicate operation on a fellow human, their curiosity can

border on peril. Sterile fields are not supposed to be disrupted by nosy monkeys.

Long-glanded coral snakes are plentiful in the Bataan jungles as well. These are venomous snakes, as are cobras, vipers, and sea snakes, all native to the area, each fully capable of completely ruining a single nurse's day in a heartbeat. Also, about twenty species of bats make their homes on the peninsula. Probably the most memorable is the giant golden-crowned "flying fox," or golden-capped fruit bat. It is one of the largest bat species in the world, weighing about three pounds and having a "forearm length" of over eight inches. Not a welcome visitor during nighttime patient checks.

Why, one might ask, would the United States Army and Navy want to take patients out into this horrid jungle with rampant malaria and potentially deadly species of snakes and many other animals all around them? The answer was clear: the Japanese wouldn't be looking for them there, and hopefully, the Americans could hold off until more troops were sent in to rescue them. And so, at Christmastime, 1941, the U.S. Army, consisting of about 20,000 Americans and 80,000 Filipino troops of all ranks and military occupations, plus about 3,000 patients, along with medical staff to care for these patients, retreated onto the Bataan Peninsula. Manila was declared an open city, and the American military forces abandoned the metropolis, leaving only civilians behind.

Another reason the evacuation to the Bataan Peninsula occurred was that there were no other options.

Six US military hospitals on Luzon were abandoned. Sally's previous hospital, Stotsenburg at Clark Field, was not severely damaged and remained open after most patients were evacuated. The severely ill and injured remained at Stotsenburg Hospital, about 50 miles north of Manila. Dedicated and resilient military staff took great risks to remain with those patients. A few brave Navy nurses also provided medical care to a small number of critically ill military patients at a converted girls' school in Manila.

Once the brick-and-mortar hospitals had been evacuated of patients and caregivers, nonmedical army and navy personnel set about removing anything and everything they could from the storerooms and all other areas of the various facilities. These supplies were moved to a warehouse near the town of Limay on the eastern coastal plains of Bataan.

On December 22, 1941, a number of nurses were sent to organize what was described as being an "outdoor" hospital. By the time the Japanese forces began their infantry attacks on the peninsula on January 7, the Americans and Filipinos had set up makeshift wards under bamboo and acacia trees in the dense jungle of Bataan.

By December 26, 1941, the first Jungle Hospital had already received its first 212 patients. On January 16, 1942, Jungle Hospital #1 performed 187 major surgical operations in 24 hours, a record far exceeding typical wartime hospitals in the US at the time.

Shortly after this first hospital was becoming a reality, the army had begun assembling a Jungle Hospital #2 at the southern portion of Bataan in an area known as Cabcaben, north of the town of Marivelles. Sally Blaine was part of this second group of nurses.

Sketch of Jungle Hospital No. One (On Next Page)

Image from the Ethel "Sally" Blaine Millett Collection

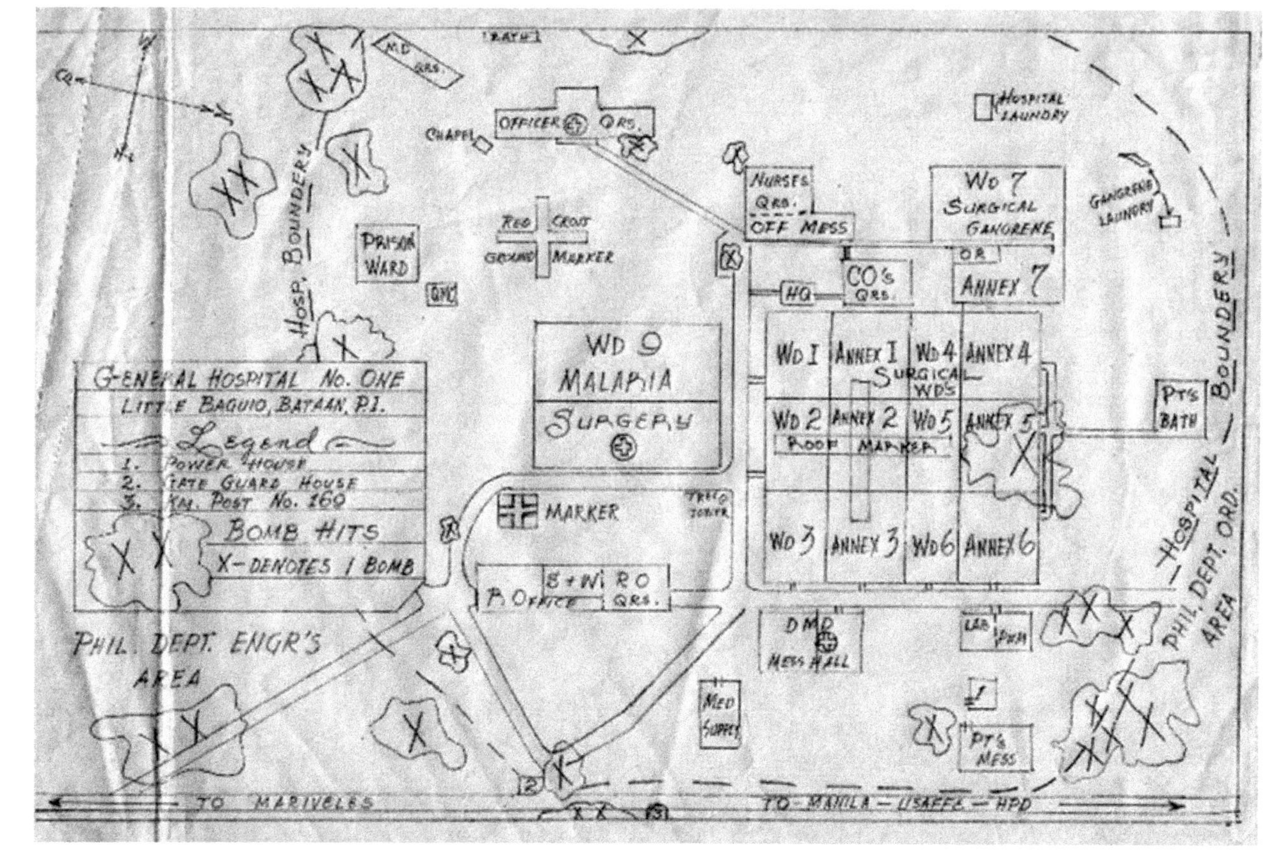

GENERAL HOSPITAL No. ONE
LITTLE BAGUIO, BATAAN, P.I.
Legend
1. Provost House
2. Little Guard House
3. Kin Post No. 169
BOMB HITS
X - DENOTES I BOMB
PHIL. DEPT. ENGR'S AREA
TO MARIVELES
TO MANILA - USAFFE - HPD
HOSP. BOUNDERY
PRISON WARD
RED CROSS GROUND MARKER
CHAPEL
OFFICER QRS.
OFFICER'S OR.
WD 9 MALARIA
SURGERY
MARKER
S + W RO QRS.
R. OFFICE QRS.
MED SUPPLY
DMD MESS HALL
HQ
CO's QRS.
OFF. MESS
NURSES QRS.
WD I ANNEX I
WD 4 ANNEX 4
WD 2 ANNEX 2
WD 5 ANNEX 5
WD 3 ANNEX 3
WD 6 ANNEX 6
SURGICAL WDS
ROOF MARKER
OR ANNEX 7
WD 7 SURGICAL GANGRENE
HOSPITAL LAUNDRY
GANGRENE LAUNDRY
PRS MESS
LAB PHM
PRS BATH
PHIL. DEPT. ORD. AREA
HOSPITAL BOUNDERY

JUNGLE TRIAGE

Start the breathing, stop the bleeding,
protect the wound and treat for shock.
Battlefield First Aid Rules

"This little sketch is the only plan we have for these jungle hospitals," said Lieutenant Colonel Frank Adamo, one of a team of Filipino and American Army officers overseeing the setup of the Bataan field hospitals. He was holding a very rough sketch indeed, drawn on a plain piece of white typing paper. The military troops on Bataan were ready to do the impossible. "This map is not much to go on," he said, "but it's all we have."

Jungle Hospital #2 was situated along a pretty river called the Reall. The medical teams were now tasked with setting up an identical hospital to #1, completed just hours before this second installation. There were 18 open-air wards capable of accommodating 300–400 patients each. The average daily census would burgeon to as many as 5,000 patients. Half of the seventy-seven US Army Nurses, assisted by nurses from the Filipino Army, would work around the clock in each of the two hospitals: Hospital No. 1 near the town of Limay, and Hospital No. 2 in the dense jungle area of Cabcaben north of the coastal town of Marivelles.

The Army Nurse Corps members were led by Captain Maude C. Davison and Second Lieutenant Josephine Nesbit. Responsibilities at all levels of hospital staff in all hospital departments were shared by both American and Filipino members of the Joint Command. Open-air wards, a practice not seen in US military hospitals since the Civil War, allowed for better ventilation but exposed patients and staff to the elements, including tropical diseases. Clear military chains of command were credited with maintaining order, efficiency, communication, and decision-making, even as the situation deteriorated. The resilience and ingenuity of the medical personnel gave testament to the quality of the personnel involved.

Lieutenant Colonel Frank Adamo began giving orders in what must have seemed to be a "fly-by-the-pants" operation. Nevertheless, Adamo provided an air of complete confidence, as if this was just part of his routine job.

"Captain Davison and Lieutenant Nesbit," Adamo said, "you set up the wards as you see on this drawing— this is my only copy, so pay attention. To begin with, we will use stretchers right on the ground to bed the patients."

And so, the assembling of this second impossible hospital began.

"From the beginning," Adama continued, "everyone must take it upon him- or herself to make things work. Everyone must conduct themselves in harmony to get the job done, even when the task seems impossible." Adamo walked among the assembled group. "There will be no grumbling regarding the challenging conditions or the necessity for creativity."

And there was no complaining. The tasks were conducted with a minimum of delays. Everyone was courteous and focused. Serious focus was needed because the first casualties arrived before the setup was even close to completion. As soon as the American and Filipino forces established lines to hold back the Japanese troops that were breathing down their necks, casualties from the battlefield were transported to the open-air medical "facilities."

The nurses walked around the trampled ground where they were told the hospital would be constructed. It was a dark December night by any standard, but under the canopy of a huge tropical jungle, the word "dark" took on new and disquieting dimensions. Even with the dimmed search lights being used to set up the hospital, it was impossible to see anything on the outer edges of the encampment. The outside perimeters lent no insight into what was beyond.

"How can it be this dark?" Sally asked some nurses by her as they unpacked and set up nurses' stations in the wards with no walls. "If I look above me, there is just more darkness. It's almost like being in a prehistoric time, especially with these jungle sounds all around us."

But following the long night when the nurses first arrived, a miraculous thing happened. The sun rose over the rain forest, and the dense black of the first night was relieved by cheerful sunlight peeking through the misty canopy of jungle growth over their heads.

"Look!" exclaimed Sally, pointing above. "It looks like a fairy land! The sun twinkles when the breeze blows through the treetops."

Work stopped for a long moment, while the exhausted nurses gazed at the beauty of the new dawn's sunlight.

There was no sleep that first night. The nurses worked quickly, quietly, and carefully, considering how close to combat the new hospital would be. About the only positive the American and Filipino militaries had in their undertaking was that dense cover of jungle that would be their constant companion on Bataan. At least the Japanese could not see the Americans and Filipinos from the air, which of course was the point of the whole operation. But just about everything else being asked of the medical staff could have been placed in the category of difficult to near impossible.

The wildlife wasn't much happier about them being there than they themselves were. A tropical jungle is a symphony of sounds from insects, birds, and animals. Squawks and trills and caws and hoots and many other unsettling sounds penetrated the quiet setting, day and night. This jungle was anything but quiet! And yet everyone was *ordered* to be as quiet as possible.

Second Lieutenant Josie Nesbit and Captain Maude Davidson could no longer "bark" orders. They learned to use a very forceful "stage whisper."

"I know the lighting is dim here, even in broad daylight, but obviously we don't want to broadcast our presence to any Japanese bombers overhead," croaked Captain Davidson. "As you nurses can see, the boundaries of Hospital No. 2 have been staked out by the engineers. We are standing about in the center of the proposed hospital. Within these boundaries, you can also see two Red Cross symbols in bright red canvas on the ground," she pointed, "one to the west of us and one to the east. These are supposed to indicate a no-bomb-area."

Second Lieutenant Nesbit continued, "Where you are standing will be the surgery bays—with another large Red Cross hung overhead—and Ward 9, the Malaria Ward. This area is just about dead center in the middle of the hospital."

Captain Davis chimed in. "Adjacent to Surgery are Wards 1 through 6, with adjacent annexes for expansion, plus a 7th Ward and Annex for Surgical and Gangrene patients. Note that there is a separate facility for gangrene laundry." There were a few raised eyebrows, but the nurses knew the importance of infection control, so no one commented. Davis continued, "The Commanding Officer's Quarters, the Nurses Quarters, and the Officers' Mess are adjacent to these wards." She paused to clear her throat. "You will eat, work, and sleep as close to your patients as possible."

Nesbit stepped up next to Davis and said, "There is one ward we have not told you about. Ward Zero is on the other side of the hospital, away from other patients for obvious reasons. This is the Prisoner Ward. The number of Zero reflects the status of the patients as captured enemy troops. They will be treated the same as our own soldiers but will be kept apart and closely guarded."

The nurses and other medical staff worked tirelessly until Hospital No. 2 was completely set up. It was not lost on the nurses that the entire operation felt like children playing make believe, imagining a great palace complete with a prince and princess with just some chalk lines drawn on the sidewalk. But the patients who had been evacuated from the military hospitals on Luzon Island were every bit as real as they had been in the brick-and-mortar buildings they came from, and new patients with more acute and catastrophic injuries began populating the beds right alongside those patients already "admitted."

The officers oversaw Sally's team of about thirty-five American nurses and an equal number of Filipino nurses who would serve at Jungle Hospital #2. There was no handbook on how to proceed. It is amazing that the staff had not only moved patients here from the brick-and-mortar hospitals, but they were also immediately receiving battle casualties from the troop line being set up along the northern end of the Bataan Peninsula. Monitoring all of this was largely a matter of trial and error on everyone's part. No hospitals the size of these two jungle hospitals had ever been put together with such speed and precision as the ones on the Bataan Peninsula.

Captain Davidson continued. "This first hospital is expected to have a capacity of around 2,900 beds organized into approximately 18 open-air wards, with each ward designed to shelter roughly 300–400 patients." Davidson paused. "For those of you who can do math in your heads,

400 patients times 18 wards come to 7,200 patients, which is a high prediction of what the census may reach in each jungle hospital here on Bataan. With thirty-five US nurses and about the same number of Filipino nurses, that means each nurse could be responsible for as many as 103 patients on a shift."

"The hospital must be built quickly using available materials," Lieutenant Nesbit continued. "Our focus will be on making things functional and preparing patient bed setups as rapidly as possible." She paused. "We need to be ready to serve patients yesterday."

"I was worried we'd get shorted on food out here in the jungle. But we are being fed just like when we left Clark!" a fellow nurse said to Sally one of the first evenings.

The meals were on par with the ones served at Stotsenberg Hospital and the nurses' barracks at Clark Army Base. But the huge kitchen, stocked well at first, would see supplies dwindle by the week. Within a short time, daily rations were reduced to three-quarter size. No one knew how long they would be in the jungle, and the commanding officers determined that food needed to be restricted.

Angelito was emptying trash in the medical teams' mess tent just as an American orderly walked by the area with a glum look on his face.

"What's wrong with him?" Angelito asked Sally.

"He got assigned to the morgue, tagging bodies," Sally answered.

"Oh, that's too bad!" he said. "But at least he will not see patients suffering."

There needed to be a morgue with plenty of body bags. Mass graves had to be dug in which to place the body bags as they inevitably accumulated. Staff needed to be assigned to each of these areas, and this young orderly had drawn the short straw.

There was also an area set up within each hospital to house those patients who were not likely to survive their injuries or illnesses. It was part of the "triage" process. When the doctors examined patients who were clearly near death with no further treatment possible, they would be moved to a special area. Nurses sat with them and kept them comfortable, often hearing their last words on this earth. The chaplains from all faiths kept a close eye on the patients there as well, coming in with Angelo in tow when he was available. The chaplains administered the last rites to the believers and spoke words of comfort to every patient they could.

Next, having enough supplies was paramount, including but not limited to surgical instruments, bandages, medications, and blood plasma. Both Filipino and American emergency medicine doctors, surgeons, nurses, orderlies, and support staff would be carrying out the tasks of the field hospital, with as close to normal protocols as possible.

The bulldozers and heavy machine operators were kept on hand to quickly beat back the jungle growth, making room for the expansion of the hospitals over time.

Ambulances without the use of sirens would transport casualties from the front line at the north and south ends of the peninsula to the emergency services and triage areas. Sometimes other vehicles were used for transport, such as delivery vans, supply trucks, or any vehicle with a working engine for troops with less severe injuries. Also, buses were needed to move troops to and from "barracks" set up in the middle of the jungle near the hospitals. The troops needed to be moved back to the war zone when they were on duty again. The natural cover of the jungle provided a relatively secure environment for treating and caring for the wounded, away from the immediate threat of enemy attacks.

In other wartime scenarios, stabilized patients were usually transported to actual hospitals with walls and floors and ceilings, via special medical helicopter or land ambulances. But there was nowhere and no way to take the patients to conventional hospitals from Bataan. All patients had to stay at the jungle hospitals until they were well enough to return to active duty. Critically ill or severely injured troops remained in patient status until the Bataan occupation ended.

Field hospitals in such a tropical environment faced incredible logistical challenges. Besides malaria, other diseases such as dengue fever, dysentery, beriberi, diarrhea, pellagra, rickets, scurvy, and vitamin and mineral deficiencies plagued both patients and staff. Mosquito nets by the thousands were procured, but not fast enough to prevent massive numbers of personnel succumbing to bites from malaria-infected mosquitoes.

EARLY PATIENT ARRIVALS

The exact timeline for when the Japanese discovered the location of the American and Filipino troops and the new field hospital is not well documented. The situation was chaotic, and the field hospital was clearly not completely set up when the first casualties were brought in. Sally and her fellow nurses learned this early on.

One day, Sally and some other nurses were trying to set up the outdoor ward as quickly and efficiently as they could. Suddenly there was a huge commotion at the north end of their open-air area. An ambulance had backed up to where the driver thought the emergency department would be located, but he was closer to where the nurses were putting away the supplies.

The ambulance driver and the emergency attendant jumped out and started yelling.

"We've got one critical soldier and three walking wounded, all in our ambulance! You've got to help us quick!"

"ER is over to the west of our station, about half a football field away!"

But the ambulance attendant had turned back around and was unloading the critically ill soldier, who looked like he was bleeding heavily from one of his legs. The "walking wounded" had also begun to climb out of the ambulance, displaying several serious and critical injuries over many body parts. None of them looked gravely injured, so Sally turned her attention back to the man on the stretcher rack that had just been unloaded from the ambulance and placed on the ground. Sally's nostrils filled with the metallic bite of iron. The blood was everywhere: on the patient's clothing, the emergency workers, the stretcher, the bandages, the ground. So much blood. Even before his clothing had been removed, Sally could see that the man had lost part of his lower leg, probably from a bomb blast. He would most likely need an amputation of the part of the leg that was still attached. Surgery was definitely imminent.

"Quick!" Sally called to the other nurses gathered nearby. "Get me scissors and bandages to replace the ones this man has bled through. We don't have time to load him back in the ambulance, and I can see a supply truck blocking the clearing by the ER area!"

When the clean bandages were brought to Sally and the ambulance attendants, they set about cutting off the bloody clothing and soiled wrappings and replacing them with clean dressings. A tourniquet had been applied by the ambulance staff, but it was doing little to stop the bleeding. The two ambulance attendants hoisted the stretcher rack by the wooden handles to their shoulders and headed in the direction of the ER area. While the men carried the patient, Sally applied hand pressure as best she could. Another nurse held the intravenous bottle aloft as they walked. The IV was started right away as soon as the patient had been loaded into the ambulance. Administering IV fluids and medications helped manage shock, dehydration, and blood loss, significantly improving the chances of survival for many soldiers.

The emergency department staff took over as soon as the ambulance workers and the nurses transported the patient across the uneven ground that served as a roadway along the northern portion of the Jungle Hospital. The walking wounded followed the medical workers, making a motley-looking procession. Sally and the other nurse were happy to turn all the patients over to their coworkers in the emergency area and return to the relative calm of taking care of recovering patients. But these types of situations were not uncommon when an emergency occurred in their wards and they needed to respond quickly, hopefully saving lives and preventing further injury or complications. A war zone is *always* a living, breathing monster with its teeth bared and its back raised, ready to inflict chaos, severe injuries, and life-threatening conditions at any time of night or day.

The medical personnel made gallant efforts to treat each new patient with skill and compassion in the early hours of the field hospitals' operation. This included the treatment of gunshot wounds, blast injuries (including limbs that needed amputation), traumatic brain injuries, fractures and dislocations, and thermal and chemical burns. Within a few days, the need for infection control mushroomed, and psychological trauma (then called "shell shock," now identified as post-traumatic stress disorder, or PTSD) was evident. The nurses had their hands full, using every skill learned in their training, as well as the fortitude to approach and treat patients with multiple medical issues under deplorable conditions. Recently developed medical advancements, such as pain medications and antibiotics, undoubtedly saved many lives and relieved much suffering. But too soon, supplies began to run out.

The Abyss, that ever-present feeling of evil, swirled around the legs of the hospital workers and combat troops, like fog in the jungle. They couldn't see the Abyss, but they felt it, like a cold, tingling sensation crawling up their legs to their spine and settling at the base of their skulls. Their dedication was secure, their sense of purpose unshakeable. But the Abyss hissed, nevertheless. "Axis of Power!" it said, over and over like a malicious mantra. The power mongers of the world were trying to stop the American and Filipino forces from prevailing.
"Axis of Power!"

HOSPITAL EXPANSION

Hospital #1 had been set up near Limoge at a place called Little Baguio, which had been a Philippine Army engineers' headquarters. Hospital Number One took over an old building inside which double-decker patient beds had been built. The doctors and nurses assigned to Hospital Number One tended to their patients inside this building.

"Jungle Hospital" was soon renamed Hospital Number Two. Sally was assigned to Hospital Number Two. In the beginning, they had no buildings. They had no double-decker beds. They had flat bivouac mattresses lying on the ground. There were no bedside tables, no chairs, no furniture at all to speak of. The only protection against the elements was a makeshift covering over the medical records.

"This is the bleakest affair I ever saw in my life," Sally said the day she arrived. Her opinion of the setup didn't change, but her attitude and actions surely did. Every nurse, from the ER to surgery to recovery to "long term" patient care, had to come to grips with the cards they were being dealt. There was no real rehabilitation for patients. They were either discharged, often way too early, and sent back to combat, or they were cared for tenderly until they left this world, or they were cared for tenderly until the Bataan campaign ended with an even more devastating outcome none could yet imagine.

Nurses Bathing in a Nearby Creek

Photographed by Annalee Whitmore photo found in the Ethel "Sally" Blaine Millett Collection.

The nurses drew water from a creek for use with their patients. The only baths given to the patients were with cold water from that creek. Water was heated for cooking, but not for bathing. The nurses and officers bathed in the same creek where they got water for their patients, and the water was just as cold. They learned early on to wash hair and bodies expediently, get out of the creek and dry off, and dress as quickly as possible.

Within a short period of time, there were eighteen wards in Hospital Number Two, strung out along a small river called the Reall. Whenever the wards all filled up, a bulldozer would come in and cut a pathway through the jungle for more patient beds. In those days, there were no heat-sensing technologies, no GPS, nothing but the very beginnings of radar technologies. The dense foliage in the Bataan region allowed the Americans and Filipinos to "hide in plain sight."

"I felt completely protected," Sally said later. "The canopy completely obliterated our view of the airplanes flying over and their view of us. I loved it! I guess what you can't see can't hurt you!"

"How can anybody expect us nurses to wear these stupid white uniforms, white caps, white shoes, and *especially* our white stockings!" one nurse wailed to her coworkers. This was soon every nurse's hew and cry to each other and to their commanding officers. "We can't possibly keep these uniforms clean out here in the jungle, and they are uncomfortable—especially the white *stockings!* Besides, the men are all wearing fatigues, from the lowest noncom to the highest-ranking general. How come *they* get to be so casual, and we have to dress to the nines?"

While taking most of the inconveniences of the jungle hospitals in stride, the nurses were particularly rattled by the fact they were expected to wear their regulation clothing "on the job" in the jungle. They had no place to change or freshen up, so most showed up in the regulation clothing they had been wearing when they left the hospital to sleep at night, and they continued to wear the uniforms day after day.

In short order, however, the commanding officers of the Nurse Corps were granted permission to requisition smaller sizes of khaki pants and shirts for the women to wear. It was no longer practical to wear white *anything*, especially in an outdoor hospital in a jungle. Thus, the nurses in the Bataan jungle hospitals became the first women in military history to wear khakis in the line of duty. Angelito performed his "procurement magic" by providing small-size khaki pants and shirts in abundance so the nurses would have plenty to choose from. No one questioned his need for the clothing, but some suspected that the smaller sizes of plain khakis came from the storehouses of the Filipino army, whose members were smaller in stature than their American counterparts. It was clear that the khakis were the only solution for the nurses who needed to be comfortable and move easily in a tropical environment.

Another change that may have been more subtle was a change in attitude for the nurses, from shift-work caregivers to "guerrilla nursing caregivers," beating back jungle vegetation as it grew like magic in and around the area where the patients lay. There seemed to be nothing—absolutely nothing—that kept the nurses from their appointed duty. No matter how hot the jungle got, no matter how few medical supplies they had to work with, the nurses brought professionalism, patience, and most of all, a special kind of healing to their patients lying in front of them on the jungle floor. There was literally no sacrifice these women were not willing to make to foster a restorative atmosphere in their "wards."

A constant dull roar continued unabated in the Bataan jungle. Most thought it was the roar of battle, and the nurses learned to tune it out. But in quiet times when they were alone trying to bathe or sleep, they were acutely aware of the precarious position they were all in. The only thing keeping the Japanese from overtaking them was a line of infantry men in hand-to-hand combat with their Japanese counterparts. The line could be broken at any time. Evil was constantly at their doorstep.

"Axis of Power!"

FRIEND BECOMES PATIENT

One day Sally sat on an old chair in the middle of her ward, trying to concentrate on her patients' care instead of her own nausea and weakness. Sally, like many other nurses, had contracted malaria, most likely from a mosquito bite from one of the billions of the little monsters that inhabited every square centimeter of the Bataan Peninsula. This particular day, a new patient was brought in with his ever-present government paperwork. He didn't sound very happy about being admitted to *any* hospital, jungle or otherwise. Sally recognized his voice and spoke to him as sternly as she could muster.

"Angelito, don't you *dare* come into *my* ward causing trouble!"

"Oh, Miss Sally!" came the reply. "Please to—how you say?—discharge me most quickly. I must get back to my job in the front."

"Well, that depends on why you were brought here in the first place!" Sally said. She addressed the orderlies who had brought Angelito to the ward.

"Why did he need to be admitted?" she asked. The orderly responded immediately.

"Well, ma'am, he has a sore on his leg that isn't healing. It got infected, and the doctor said he needs to stay off the leg for a while to allow it to heal properly. Otherwise, he may have worse trouble down the road."

"I'm fine!" Angelito protested. "I can walk on the leg, see?" He tried to get up off the gurney, but he promptly fell to the ground.

"Not so fast, there, soldier!" Sally said, as she and the orderly caught him before he collapsed completely. "That wound must be pretty bad if you can't stand on it!"

"Just give me a shot of morphine for the pain, and I'll be good as new!" Angelito protested.

The orderly spoke up. "Soldier, the doctor said you could get an infection in the wound and then you'd be in real trouble. You might even get gangrene, and we are running low on mercury compounds and iodine to treat that. So, there might not be anything to heal your wound if it gets worse."

"Listen to what we are saying, Angelito. Please just let that leg heal," Sally said. "They will survive without you on the front for a few days."

Reluctantly, Angelito had to listen to Sally because he respected her. He knew gangrene was a very dangerous infection and he didn't want to find out the hard way how perilous it could be. Besides, the nurses pampered him and shared with him their precious chocolate stashes and goodies sent from their families in the States.

And he could use a little rest…

In 1941, Christmas Eve and Christmas Day saw the jungle hospitals being set up and the medical personnel getting back to the business of helping the wounded and ill soldiers heal. Any mention of the sacred holiday was only in passing. There were no real gifts shared, although some creative members of the team made efforts to remember their fellow nurses, doctors, orderlies, and other staff. Simple handmade gifts were exchanged, and friends honored each other with handwritten notes. There was no Christmas feast. In fact, the cooks had precious little to work with.

The census in each of the two jungle hospitals continued to grow. Every nurse was needed on a regular schedule at the hospitals.

By Sally's birthday, February 19, 1942, she was a charge nurse, supervising a ward full of nurses and patients. She was already very sick with malaria and too weak to stand for any length of time, but she didn't want to let her patients down. She had a cot moved to the center of the outdoor ward, and she lay on the cot and gave orders to her nurses. When she wasn't scheduled to work, she lay on her pallet in the little open-air encampment she shared with other nurses. On her birthday, while she was at work resting on her cot at the hospital, a Navy officer came through. He was on his way to visit one of his men in the hospital. He overheard Sally giving instructions to the nurses.

"I'll never forget him," Sally said. "He looked straight at me."

"My. You look like a sick cat," the man said. "You look like you could use some food. Could you?"

Sally answered weakly, "Yes, maybe I could."

Then he left. But he came back the next day.

"He brought me cheese, crackers, and candy," Sally told the others. It was so unexpected, and even though the man came back the day after Sally's birthday, she thought it was a very nice birthday present. She was sure she'd never see the man again because she and other nurses had heard that they soon would be moved to the island of Corregidor.

PENTHOUSE TO BUNKER

*J*eanne Marie Faircloth had always been accustomed to "creature comforts." Born in Nashville, Tennessee, in 1898 to a wealthy southern banker, Jeanne's parents divorced when she was eight. Jean understood from early on that both sides of her family hailed from aristocratic southern roots, had access to great wealth and all its trappings, and could boast of generations of military service, back to the Confederate Army and before. Jean loved all things military. It seemed that her meeting and falling in love with a man eighteen years her senior, General Douglas MacArthur, was a match made in heaven. She was just the kind of woman MacArthur would have chosen years before, if such an opportunity had presented itself.

Jeanne was a petite woman, but fearless and confident enough in herself to be traveling alone from New York City to Shanghai in 1937. Another passenger on her ship was General MacArthur, bound for the Philippines. Jean decided to skip Shanghai and got off at Manila, where MacArthur also disembarked. She and the general were married two years later in New York, during MacArthur's trip home to build support for the defense of the

Philippines. The general had retired from the United States Army in 1937 but become a Philippine Army field marshal advising the Philippine government in preparation for their upcoming July 4, 1946, independence from the United States.

Quiet and composed, Jeanne served as a backdrop and constant support for her husband, and she closely shielded the family's private life. The couple lived their days in service to the people of the Philippines and the United States. When their only child was born, Arthur MacArthur IV, named after his paternal grandfather, the parents doted on him and raised him in a loving—and of course structured—environment.

How could this be, now, that this family, emergent from money and privilege, found themselves moving to an underground bunker on the Philippine Island of Corregidor, or "The Rock," as it was called? How could they decide what to reasonably take, or more importantly, leave behind—of their seemingly limitless possessions? China and silver? What use would they be? Fine glassware and linens? The Japanese bombing broke tougher glass products than theirs, and the Malinta Tunnel's ceiling shed fine particles of concrete dust each time the enemy fired mortars at the ground above. And what of little four-year-old Arthur's toys (mostly military trucks and ships and flying machines)? How could he play with them on a cold concrete floor in whichever portion of "the third lateral tunnel from the east entrance" they would be

calling home? But Jean Macarthur squared her shoulders, took a deep breath, and resolved not to complain about their new accommodations. Her husband was the high command of this crazy mission. He was determined to keep the American and Filipino hospital staff and patients, as well as the soldiers fighting on the front line, as safe as possible until American troops came to their rescue. The sooner the better, Jeanne thought, though neither she nor her husband truly knew if that rescue would take place at all. She was determined to do her part, no matter the cost, to support her husband and keep her son occupied. But their time on Corregidor was short lived. On March 11, 1942, under direct orders from President Franklin D. Roosevelt, MacArthur with his wife and son made a harrowing journey by PT boat through Japanese-controlled waters to the island of Mindanao, a trip of several hours when not dodging enemy combatants. From Mindanao, the family flew to safety of Australia. His departure was part of a broader strategy to prevent his capture by the Japanese and to allow him to reorganize Allied forces from a safe place. Many thought MacArthur's departure had a devastating effect on morale of the troops left behind.

GET IT RIGHT THE FIRST TIME

By the first of April 1942, all of the nurses, most ill with malaria and other tropical diseases, had been ordered off the peninsula and into the Malinta Tunnel on the nearby island of Corregidor. Not one of the nurses asked to go, and several of them told their superior officers they wanted to stay with their patients in the jungle. The nurses, even the sickest among them, were distressed about what kind of care the patients would receive if the women all left. The American and Filipino doctors (all male, some also ill with dengue fever and malaria) were not being evacuated yet, but the nurses argued in vain that, without their ability to maintain the bonds they developed with so many patients, those patients would suffer tremendously.

Henry David Thoreau said, *"Could a greater miracle take place than for us to look in each other's eyes for just an instant?"* The circumstances the American and Filipino health care teams found themselves in at the jungle hospitals seem impossible to imagine. But these nurses regarded each of their patients with empathy, humility, and honor. They *"looked into their eyes"* and saw each one as a distinct human being with a life *before* Bataan, and hopefully a life *after*. Some of these men were gravely injured, many to the point where their lives would never be the same. The nurses cared for them, cried with them, grieved with them, listened to them rage about the folly of war, and soothed them into troubled but still somewhat restful sleep. Each nurse was the best friend to her individual patients, no matter how sad, depressed, injured, ill, angry, or selfish the soldier became.

Everyone who was still on Bataan realized the Japanese were closing in on the US and Philippine troops who still held the front line to the north. The casualties they were seeing were coming in faster, and with shrinking supplies and medications, the opportunities to treat the patients were disappearing fast. They all waited and prayed for General MacArthur to announce that *help really was on the way*. But after three and a half months in the steaming jungle with dwindling food, medicine, and other provisions, it was the nurses who kept the patients on track to recovery by validating their fear, anxiety, pain (both physical and emotional), and worry. A patient was more than his chart, his diagnosis, his treatment plan, or even his military experience. Much of the nurses' time was spent "connecting" to each patient, understanding, "seeing" (and treating) the whole person and building trust.

"It is absolutely essential," Sally told the nursing staff under her charge, "that we *get it right the first time* with each one of our patients."

These praise-worthy practices by the nurses were what also held those amazing women close to each other. Mutual support was a key factor in the nurses' mental stability during the most unsettling of conditions. They *got it right the first time and every time* with each other too.

By early April 1942, there were at least 4,000 patients in Hospital #2 alone, a space set up for a maximum of 2,000 patients. But the nurses were "soldiers" too, and the day came when they were ordered to be evacuated to Corregidor. And what a nightmare that evacuation was!

ANGEL TEARS

The dark black night descended on hospital #2 in the Bataan jungle, and with it the Abyss of cold fear and impossible expectations. The canopy of foliage engulfed the sky, except for occasional open spaces between the high, dense branches. The stars shone so brightly through those gaps some nights that their beauty made Sally want to cry. Angelito said the stars were "angel tears" from the residents of heaven who were weeping for the awful conditions the nurses faced every time they came to work on one of the concrete wards of Corregidor.

The black nights of the jungle used to make Sally feel uneasy, but her fear had long since been replaced by a profound sadness. *Does death hurt more in war, because of the futility and injustice of it all?* she thought one night. *How stupid that men and women die because their leaders cannot come to an agreement of how to live together!* She felt shame because of her longing for the meager possessions she left behind in Manila. What had happened to her dream of living in a tropical paradise? When at night she finally went to the area where the nurses slept on their cots, Sally sometimes wondered if Angelito's prayers were the only things that kept her from completely unraveling.

Sally never cried. When her heart ached, she thought first of her patients, and then her fellow nurses and other medical staff. And last her family back in Missouri. Would she ever see them again?

There was only one action to be taken, and that was to rest when she could (with her mosquito net firmly secured around her cot), and return to duty ready to administer her nursing skills to those who needed them.

As a charge nurse, Sally was responsible for the day-to-day treatment and care of over a thousand patients, numbers that were burgeoning relentlessly. The responsibility each nurse had would have been considered shockingly unfair in a stateside hospital or an ordinary military medical installation anywhere else in the world. Sometimes Sally and the other nurses would talk about how they got here, to this unimaginable situation of creating a "hospital"—if one could call it that—in the middle of this senseless war. But all any of them could do was put one foot in front of the other and do the job they were assigned.

A Bit of Well-Needed Humor at the Bataan Nurses' Quarters
*National Museum of the U.S. Navy—Office of War Information
Photograph, 9-15 April 1942. Photo found in the Ethel "Sally"
Blaine Millett Collection.*

COLLATERAL DAMAGE

"Collateral damage" was a catch phrase in the halls of the 77th Congress of the United States of America in early 1942. The Washington "fat cats"—the Senators and congressional representatives from 1941 to 1943—included a hundred and twenty-one men and ten women. Prior to entering the war, the United States Congress and the populace were bitterly divided over issues such as the New Deal and whether to intervene in the conflict erupting in Europe. "Isolationists" wanted nothing to do with helping other countries fight their battles. "Interventionists" or "Internationalists" thought assisting European nations against Hitler and Mussolini would prevent destabilization of the World Order. But the US was quickly involved in multiple conflicts soon after President Roosevelt declared war on Japan following the horrific and unforeseen bombing of Pearl Harbor, Hawaii, by the Japanese.

"We must prioritize our resources," argued those who saw value in combining forces with European nations. "Our military is stretched thin, and we must address the most crucial threats." "Hitler in Germany and Mussolini in Italy are our fiercest opponents in this war, and we

must direct the bulk of our war chest into those theaters."
"We must focus on defeating the Axis powers in Europe and the Pacific."

"There is no time to run a rescue operation in the Philippines! They are too far away, and they are not as central to American defense positions as European interests. Besides, we have no military base in the Bataan Peninsula, so it is futile to think the troops there can be saved in a reasonable manner. They must be written off as 'collateral damage!'"

"Collateral damage."

The American and Filipino ground troops never thought they might be considered "collateral damage" as they held off the Japanese on the northern edge of the Bataan Peninsula in the four months following Christmas Eve 1941. The situation was dire from the beginning, and it was nothing short of a miracle that the Japanese were initially unable to break through that fragile line. But there was so much at stake, and the American and Filipino forces never considered failure as an option. The number of patients in jungle hospitals #1 and #2 had burgeoned to unmanageable numbers, with new "wards" being created weekly. Each time more soldiers fell and were brought to the outdoor emergency "rooms," a bulldozer would arrive to make room for more patients. The hospitals were running out of medical supplies and medicines. Without enough mosquito nets for all patients, let alone staff, malaria, dengue fever, and yellow fever were winning the infection battle. Cases were rampant.

After General Douglas MacArthur took his family and left for Australia, his absence was met with anger, bitterness, and in many cases, unforgiveness from those he believed he was serving the best way he could. He promised to return but did not do so until the damage was done, and the war was over. The staff of jungle hospitals #1 and #2 were trying desperately to keep going just one more day. They were hungry and emaciated but still doing what they always did, just going to work under the worst of conditions. The needs of their patients came first.

But Washington refused to appropriate any funding that might have been used to save the troops and medical staff and patients on Bataan and Corregidor. "Collateral damage." There was no "cavalry" set to ride in and rescue everyone. Washington didn't seem to care much about a pretty, brown-haired nurse named Sally Blaine from Bible Grove, Missouri.

Sally too was "collateral damage."

EMERGENCY EVACUATION ARMY STYLE

"Hi, kid, fancy meeting you here!"

It was that man again, the one who gave Sally the cheese and crackers and candy on her birthday, less than three months previous. Sally perked up.

The man came out of the airplane some of the nurses were supposed to fly on. In fact, there was a last-minute announcement that several planes would be available for the nurses to board that would take them all the way to the safe shores of Australia. Sally was standing some distance from the plane, and she couldn't see the man well because it was nighttime. After the man gave Sally a hearty wave and called out to her, he began helping several nurses onto the plane. Sally kind of froze.

That man is kind of good looking, Sally said to herself.

Oh, PLEASE look at me! Sally thought. She didn't want to shout out and make a spectacle of herself. All the nurses couldn't get on the first evacuation plane. But if he would just look her way...if he would just see her, maybe, maybe by chance he would call to her and let her go to the head of the line. *C'mom, mister! See me! Remember me!*

But the man just kept loading the nurses, one by one, giving their duffle bags and any other belongings they wished to stow to a baggage handler who was packing them into a hold under the airplane's cabin.

The man never looked Sally's way again. He was being just as much a helpful gentleman to each of the nurses boarding his plane as he was to Sally when he brought Sally the cheese and crackers. She began to feel...well, put out! *How could he be so nice to ALL the nurses?* Sally thought. *I thought he kinda liked me! Wait...am I...JEALOUS?* Sally brought herself up short and thought how ridiculous that feeling was! They were in a stupid war! There was no time for silly feelings like *jealousy*!

But that plane was bound for Mindanao, with plans to have a larger plane waiting to take the women to the safety of US military bases in Australia. It was the only plane on the landing strip just outside the thick vegetation, and as far as the rest of the nurses knew, it might be the only plane the army sent to take sixty-plus nurses to safety.

That aircraft held twelve.

The remaining nurses stood in the dark, seeing the airplane taxi and take off. They watched the lights of the plane until it disappeared into the silent, inky night. Now, they marveled at the many stars, the ones they had not seen in four months, the ones that had been obscured by their constant companion, the dense, leafy ceiling of their jungle abode.

Sally never saw the nice man again. She stood with the group of nurses still waiting on the landing strip. To make things more frustrating, the unofficial word was that any nurses who could not get passage on the first plane should ride the buses—which were nowhere to be seen—down to the tip of the peninsula and catch some form of floating craft over to Corregidor. It proved to be a very long night, with only wooden benches with no backs inside the tiny building next to the airstrip. The girls could not sleep, so they tried to pass the time playing cards or telling old jokes, most of which they had all heard before.

"I sure wish we had all been able to get on a plane," Sally said, "That would have been swell. By now we would be on a transport plane direct to Australia. But now, we don't know what's to become of us!"

"Look!" another nurse said. "The sun is coming up! Let's go watch it. We haven't seen a sunrise or a sunset since…December!"

They all stood up, wriggled out the creaks in their tired bones, and piled through the door to see the sun. And magnificent it was! A fog was lifting from Manila Bay, which made the sun seem to shimmer as it rose. The sky went from dark blue through a series of pinks and oranges, until at last the day had dawned with a perfect bluebird canopy. The nurses cheered when the sun finally found its way into the spectacular sky above. A sight to behold after so many months in the jungle.

The buses did not appear, and the women were tired of waiting. Sally and others began trying to locate land transportation to the town of Mariveles. There they could get boat transportation from the peninsula to the island of Corregidor. The theory was that the troops, including the remaining nurses, would be safer from the Japanese down in the tunnels under the huge slab of rock on which Corregidor sat.

After they began to ask questions of the men at the airstrip, they were told to walk to the motor pool headquarters in a different building. They waited there only a short time, and then Sally and a few others were told to go get into a sedan and a driver would join them shortly. Five women, each with a duffel bag of belongings, could hardly fit in a sedan, but they were determined to try. When three stuffed themselves into the back seat and one got in front, another said she would ride on the running board. The driver showed up shortly, a captain wearing fatigues. The nurses should have saluted him, but the only one who wasn't squished inside the car was the woman standing on the running board. As she attempted a smart salute, the captain saluted her quicky and said, "At ease!" He never introduced himself or asked for the names of the nurses. He just climbed into the driver's seat, started the car, and off they went. The girls gave each other sidelong glances showing their increasing frustration with the way things were going this morning. By this time in this heinous war, they were all wise enough to understand that any single Japanese plane could just happen to fly over the south end of the peninsula and blow the little sedan and its passengers into tiny pieces scattered all over the road, the ditch, the treetops, and the surrounding countryside. Just one Japanese plane.

Only a short distance down the road this time, the captain stopped the car. Actually, the car stopped itself because it ran out of gas. All the nurses climbed out of the car and began walking toward the pier at Mariveles, about six miles away. They only walked about fifty yards and another sedan pulled up beside them and stopped.

"Hey," called the driver, also a captain in fatigues. "I can take some of you, but not all of you."

Now three girls piled into this next car, and the same girl said she'd ride on the running board. Some men had gotten out of the car to allow the women to ride, and the fifth girl in the group said she knew one of those men, so she would walk with them.

This second car took all day to make the trip. First, they had to stop because there was a munitions storage facility being destroyed so it would not fall into Japanese hands if the Imperial Army succeeded in capturing the remaining troops, patients, and medical staff on the Bataan Peninsula. The munitions crew had orders to destroy the ammo, and all the troops were thought to have passed by already on their way to Corregidor. But here was the car Sally was riding in, having to be halted just in time *to avoid being blown to bits, this time by her own army.*

Now the nurses were clearly ticked off. This second captain just took all of this in stride, as if this sort of craziness happened every day in the Philippines during a war between the United States and Japan. Nothing to grouse about here. Just common, everyday stuff. To be safe, the nurses walked some distance from the munitions site, sitting down near a clear running creek, under some Bani trees, blooming with fragrant white, purple, and pink flowers. If they had to wait someplace and try not to be too near the munitions pile, this was a lovely place to be.

They had to talk in between the planned explosions of all the munitions. One nurse began, "Isn't this a hoot? We were told we would get on a plane this morning and be bound for Australia. But here we are, in more danger than if we had stayed at the jungle hospitals!"

BOOM!

"Yeah, and not *one* of us wanted to leave there in the first place!"

"I *know*! We *all* said we wanted to stay and take care of our patients until the bitter end!"

BOOM! KABOOM!

"Yes, we did...but maybe we didn't realize how bad it might get if the Japanese broke through the line! We could have all been killed—or *worse*. I shudder to think what those Japanese men might have done to us American women. Remember what they did to the Chinese women at Nankin?"

KABOOM! BOOM BOOM BOOM!!!

"Well, our two drivers have been a couple of stooges!" Sally declared. "I wanted to strangle that first guy! He had to know his gas tank was nearly empty when we took off!"

The girls had to wait three hours for the men to make sure all the ammo had been exploded. By this time, their ears were ringing loudly. Later, someone told Sally there had been an earthquake near Mariveles around that time, but Sally wasn't sure she believed it. And what difference did it make what shook everyone up? The girls were all getting tired of this "evacuation" procedure. It seemed as if whoever planned this "strategy" had better go back to the drawing board.

"They thought everyone had already passed by the ordinance plant," Sally reported later. "They knew the nurses had begun their evacuation at 8:30 in the evening, but the transportation was so slow, we just crept along at a snail's pace!"

And they still were not evacuated from the peninsula. Such was the way of the military. Sometimes things fell together beautifully, and other times, well, you just had to go with the flow.

"Wait! I've lost my barracks bag!" Sally cried. "It fell off the fender into the ditch. It's all my belongings, all that's left anyway. Can't you turn around? Or slow down so I can run back and get it?"

The group had started on the way again, secure in the knowledge that the munitions had been destroyed. They could not get everyone's baggage in the sedan again, or in the trunk. Many cars in the 1940s had a depression between the front fender and hood. Someone had placed Sally's bag in that space, but the road was so bumpy, the bag worked its way out and bounced off, rolling into a ditch on the side of the road.

"Please, please, stop. That's my clothes, let me get my clothes!" By this time, Sally had lost all patience with the driver, even if he did outrank her. *He is being just plain horrible,* Sally thought. She bit her tongue and forced herself not to start shouting at him. *He could write me up,* she thought, *and worse, he probably already thinks we are inferior to him in all ways. Why show my anger and be assured he will think that way? Still, I'd sure like to crown him one!*

Sally was beginning to realize that chivalry was dead in the army. The captain didn't offer to help Sally get her clothes, but he did stop the car. Sally wormed her way out of the car and ran as fast as she could to grab the bag and get back before the captain decided to continue. The captain leisurely got out too and went to a little stream to get some water for the car's radiator. Sally had plenty of time to get back to the car, this time holding the big duffel in her lap for the rest of the trip. The captain stopped three more times, each time at a small stream so he could pour more water into the radiator. But he never asked Sally if she got her bag, and Sally was angry and discouraged at the way he ignored her completely. She sulked silently, but she could sense that her sister nurses were also angry at the captain for his obvious disdain for the female members of this chaotic mess called War Plan Orange-3. *The sooner we get off this peninsula the better*, Sally thought. *I just want someplace outside of the jungle to lay my head down and sleep tonight.*

The tired, dirty, nervous, disappointed little group of nurses was not in the mood to cheer when their driver finally pulled up to the pier at Mariveles. The nurses expected to be on a plane bound for Australia or some form of land and boat transportation to get to Corregidor Island before dawn. It took two different drivers in two different vehicles from 8:00 p.m. the previous night until close to dawn two mornings later to go less than 10 miles. When they got to the pier, there were no boats, no activity, no passengers waiting.

A couple of workers were lounging by the water, taking a break from their jobs at the pier. Sally yelled at one of them.

"Hey, you! Do you know anything about a boat for the nurses to go to Corregidor?"

"Oh, yes," said one man. "It came and went a long time ago."

Sally's heart sank. First, they had not been able to board the plane to fly to Australia. Then they had to walk to the motor pool, and the first driver ran out of gas. The second driver wouldn't stop when Sally's bag fell off the fender, and no one they had dealt with seemed to know what was going on! They could see lights on the island of Corregidor not far away from where they were standing, but what were they supposed to do to get there? Swim?

The man who said the boat left for Corregidor "a long time ago" followed Sally back to where the other nurses were standing. He knew the senior nurse in their group. They came from the United States on the same troop ship the year before.

"I've got a smaller boat that will hold five, including me," he said.

The five nurses discussed the situation and decided which one would stay behind. The bags and the people all got on the small boat and began making their way across the channel. The waves were splashing into the little boat, but not enough to dump them all into the water. Sally remembered for years afterward how beautiful that little island looked on that boat trip. As the morning dawned—for the second time during their evacuation—everything was silvery gold: the island itself and the water and the sky.

"Look at that wonderful view!" Sally shouted above the sound of the boat motor. She watched the other nurses in their little boat all turn toward "the Rock." They had seen the same beautiful sight that she had. Just as she had marveled at the pre-dawn sky peeking through the jungle canopy that first morning on Bataan, Sally again saw beauty where there had been only dismal fear and discouragement the moment before.

No fog this time around. Just an old rocky crag sticking out of Manila Bay, transformed by the breathtaking light of that early dawn and the sky becoming the clear, cerulean blue that matched the waters surrounding the Philippine Archipelago.

Corregidor was nicknamed "the Rock" because of its rocky terrain. That morning, the Rock was clothed in a gilded robe. It was impossible to tell where the water ended and the sky began. The Rock appeared to be floating somewhere in between. The nurses knew that they were being evacuated to Corregidor because it was very likely the Japanese would overcome the American and Philippine troops on Bataan soon. Their commanding officer, General MacArthur, was long gone, and nobody was coming to rescue anybody. They were on their own. But that morning, Sally would always remember the natural beauty all around them, and it was hard to believe at that moment that they were in any danger.

It was a short trip to the pier on the island, and the little group of nurses got there safe and sound, including the one who stayed behind. The man with the boat returned to pick her up and bring her back within a short time. Some people had not lost their humanity.

The Malinta Tunnel was completed in 1932 to serve as a bomb-proof shelter for military personnel and for ordnance storage. Because Corregidor and the Malinta Tunnel had been a US Army installation, there were already administrative buildings, a base exchange and commissary, a movie theater, a barber shop, and many more buildings to serve the needs of and to entertain US and Filipino troops stationed there. The island was home to dozens of tropical plants and trees, a refreshing backdrop for the austere structures used by the troops on the military bases. And unlike on the rainforest peninsula, the beautiful blue sky was visible everywhere above, without a cloud to be found that morning.

But Sally, the other nurses, and all the American and Philippine troops were not here to staff the hospital and other buildings "topside." They were on Corregidor so they could escape the enemy's advances and be safe if—when the Japanese would claim victory. The nurses' place of employment for the army was inside the sprawling Malinta tunnel where patients were being transferred now, a few at a time. After their arrival at the pier on Corregidor, the nurses found land transportation to the mouth of the great tunnel system.

Another group of nurses arrived after Sally's group, and they reported a similar experience in getting the man with the small boat to take them over the channel a few at a time. In fact, small groups of nurses arrived all day long, talking incessantly about what a horrible "evacuation" they had experienced. Some reported being strafed by bullets from Japanese planes flying low over the little boat. Luckily no one was hurt, but that was the closest the nurses had come to being part of the very real war raging all around them. When they reached what would serve as their barracks, they were relieved to have arrived but mostly disappointed at the drab setting inside Corregidor's big "Rock."

By April 9, 1942, all American and Filipino women had been safely evacuated from the Bataan jungle to the relative safety and security of Corregidor Island. Not one of those women chose to leave Bataan. They all wanted to stay with their patients, even if surrender looked imminent. But they had to obey orders. They got out in the nick of time. Bataan fell to the Japanese troops *the same day* the last nurses left. American and Filipino troops surrendered while the nurses were being ferried, a few at a time, to the Rock.

THE INEVITABLE

The ammunition was almost gone. The jungle terrain was unforgiving, growing right before the men's eyes as they fought to defend their positions. The American and the Philippine Commonwealth Forces were slowly starving while rapidly dwindling in numbers from deaths, combat injuries, and tropical diseases. They were almost thoroughly spent. It was nothing short of a miracle that they had held out against the enemy for close to four months. It seemed like four decades.

And then the inevitable happened.

The Allied forces were suddenly surrounded by enemy soldiers with guns, bayonets, swords, and knives. American and Filipino soldiers silently succumbed to the Imperial Forces, going down to defeat in what seemed like only moments. The battle ended with the surrender of Major General Edward P. King to Japanese General Masaharu Homma on April 9, 1942, one hundred and six days from the Christmas Eve the first Americans arrived on the Bataan Peninsula. General King fully understood it was not what General MacArthur and President Truman would have wanted him to do. US troops never surrendered. But he had no choice.

Instantly, 12,000 Americans and 63,000 Filipinos became prisoners of war.

The Battle of Bataan is remembered for the bravery and resilience of the Allied forces despite overwhelming odds.

The Japanese could not keep so many prisoners on the Bataan Peninsula, with no camps in which to retain them. Instead, the decision was made to force the prisoners to *march* sixty-three miles from the peninsula to numerous prison camps already in operation on the island of Luzon, where both Bataan and Manila were located. Many of those prisoners were ill and injured, including amputees and those suffering mightily from tropical diseases like malaria, dengue, yellow fever, and dysentery. Those who could not stand or walk were carried in hastily constructed blanket slings or supported by able-bodied companions. If prisoners were dropped or accidentally fell to the ground, the Japanese just shot them and left them to bleed to death as the others were forced to move past, unable to render any assistance. Sometimes the fallen were beheaded. The prisoners were made to march through tropical conditions, enduring heat, humidity, and rain without proper medical care. They suffered from starvation, having to sleep on the ground in the harsh conditions of the jungle. Filipinos suffered disproportionately worse than US troops. Seventy-one percent of the US and Filipino troops survived the march itself, but many were subjected to further harsh treatment and starvation in the Japanese prisoner-of-war camps. Some were later transported to Japan and other locations as forced laborers, enduring additional suffering on what were known as "hell ships."

The Bataan Death March stands out as one of the most brutal events of the treatment of prisoners of war in all of history.

"...with broken heart and head bowed in sadness but not in shame, I report today I must arrange terms for the surrender of the fortified islands of Manila Bay— Please say to the nation that my troops and I have accomplished all that is humanly possible and that we have upheld the best traditions—With profound regrets and with continued pride in my gallant troops, I go to meet the Japanese Commander."

General John Mayhew Wainright's Message to President Roosevelt, May 6, 1942
PIL-AMERICAN DEFENDERS, BATAAN-CORREGIDOR

General John Mayhew Waynright's Message to President Roosevelt, May 6, 1942 after the Fall of Bataan
Image from the Ethel "Sally" Blaine Millett Collection

HALLOWEEN IN APRIL

By the time Sally and the other nurses got to Corregidor, all of them had lost or misplaced many of their personal items. Miraculously, Sally's precious cosmetic bag was saved, but life in the Malinta Tunnel offered nothing that would cause the nurses to dress up and put on makeup. As they did in the jungle, they donned clean army fatigues and reported for duty. Everyone went right to work taking care of patients who were pouring in now, just like in Hospitals Number One and Number Two before the nurses left Bataan. There was no break in the action. The nurses, doctors, orderlies, and other staff operated a hospital underground in the Tunnel, becoming immune to the bombs falling above them. The worst was when the ground shook and concrete dust and even small chunks would land near a patient being tended by a nurse, or during a surgery in which it was almost impossible to keep a true "sterile field" around the patient's incision. It was bad enough just to put up with raining plaster, but when a fruit bat flew through the open gate of the West Entrance, around the tunnel system, and into a surgery bay, the poor patient had to have his procedure paused while the bat was caught and escorted outside.

The nurses had hoped that the sanitary conditions in the Malinta tunnel might have been a step up from the barest of primitive surroundings in the jungle. But when they arrived, they found the facilities to be very basic. Plumbing did not lend itself to a bomb-proof bunker, nor to a 1,000-plus-bed underground hospital. The sanitary facilities were not conducive to personal luxury. Medical staff made do with makeshift latrines and simple accommodations. Overcrowding and impossible ventilation meant more widespread disease. Under a new set of deplorable conditions, the nurses and other medical staff soldiered on. Yes, they were sometimes discouraged, and they often succumbed to anger about the situation. But their anger was for the suffering of their patients, and not the conditions under which they themselves labored.

Business went on as usual, with grueling long days for the nurses, caring for critically ill patients, using rapidly dwindling medical supplies, with worn shoes on a concrete floor. Their legs ached from the unforgiving surface. Arrangements were being made to evacuate all the nurses as soon as possible before Corregidor suffered the same fate as the jungle hospitals and front-line soldiers, now just hours away from their ultimate fate.

The Malinta Tunnel on Corregidor Island has over 24 lateral tunnels that branch off its main passageway. The project got its name as it was being built in 1922: the crew found the dirt they dug filled with leeches. The Filipino word "malinta," meaning "many leeches," seemed appropriate.

Now home to thirty-some nurses, it seemed the Tunnel was infected with more than leeches. In the dark, damp system of concrete tunnels, there were many areas in the shadows where uncomfortable thoughts resided: discouragement, fear, debilitating exhaustion, and defeat, to name a few. The tunnels reminded some of a Halloween "fun house" where scary creatures lurked at every corner, just waiting to jump out and scare someone.

It was crystal clear now that the American forces were not coming to save the Bataan and Corregidor staff and patients. The Philippines, in all its beauty and wonder and golden sunrises, was strategically off the table for help from US forces.

DEATH OF AN ANGEL

"Sally!" one of the nurses called urgently. "I thought you might want to know that Angelito was just brought into the first emergency room near the east entrance of the tunnel, closest to the triage area in the lateral tunnels."

"What? Angelito? I thought he was still in the jungle with the other men."

"It sounded like he escaped somehow, but the ER staff said it was hard to understand him. He's in pretty bad shape, Sally."

"Bad shape? How did he get here?"

"It seemed as if he got from Mariveles to Corregidor on some sort of raft he constructed."

"Well, was he shot? Or what?"

"No, it's his leg. Looks like gangrene has set in and he's in and out of consciousness."

"Oh, my goodness!" Sally exclaimed. "I wonder if I can see him."

"You'd better go fast. It doesn't look like he's got much time."

Sally took off running to the ER where she thought he might be. She asked for him by name, and she was directed to a patient bay behind a curtain. It was true, Angelito was barely coherent. When he heard her voice, he spoke so softly she could hardly hear him.

"Miss Sally, it is my leg. It is turning black now. The jungle has..."

"Don't try to talk, Angelito. It's okay."

She looked pleadingly at the doctor.

"He is a friend, Doctor. Can you save him?"

"Angelito is a friend to us all, Nurse. He is in really poor shape. We are triaging a number of patients here now, so we will have to see..."

Sally knew that meant they might not have the medicine to help him, or they might not have enough surgeons to amputate his leg. She knew what was in store by the way the doctor shook his head. Angelito probably wasn't going to make it.

She leaned down and spoke to him again.

"Angelito, does the army have your mother's address?"

With great effort, Angelito tried to hold himself up with one elbow. But he fell back onto the gurney.

"Yes..." was all he could manage. Then he reached up and tried to take off the crucifix from around his neck. "Miss Sally," he said softly, "please take...my chain...I want you...to have it."

"You mean your dog tags? No, Angelito, you need to keep them." Sally knew that might be the only way the Philippine Army could identify him and get word to his mother...

"No, no," Angelito said. "I want you...to have...the crucifix." He was out of breath, but he kept trying to get the chain from around his neck. "Help me...Miss Sally..."

Reluctantly, Sally took the silver chain and the beautiful crucifix from his neck and gently lowered his head back down on the pillow. She held it in her hand as she watched Angelito lose consciousness again...or so she thought. The doctor spoke again.

"He has been mumbling when he loses consciousness, but no one can tell if he's saying anything in particular," he said.

"Oh, we know what he's saying," explained one of the ER nurses. "He's reciting the names of every nurse he knows from working with us all these months. With his last breath, he is praying for us. For every one of us."

Sally turned to look at the nurse who uttered these amazing words. When she turned back toward Angelito, the doctor was pulling the sheet up over his face.

"Time of death," the doctor whispered, "2:36 p.m. April 10, 1941."

Sally touched his forehead gently before she stumbled from Angelito's bed, still clutching his crucifix in her hand. She began walking, but she wasn't aware where she was headed. She ended up in one of the deserted corridors of the massive Malinta Tunnel. She was silently crying now, and she heard muffled cries somewhere nearby. Was it an echo? She didn't think she had uttered anything out loud, yet there was someone making a sound.

They were not her own cries! There was someone else here. Then she heard the voices of at least two women, sobbing softly, speaking to each other.

"Who's there?" Sally asked into the dimly lit corridor.

Two nurses emerged from the darkness. The three women hugged each other and spoke softly about Angelito's passing. They all acknowledged how they were shocked and deeply saddened by his death.

ELMER'S GLUE AND
ARMY BLANKETS

Sally and the other nurses weren't on Corregidor Island long. On April 29th, two seaplanes arrived to evacuate the remaining nurses and some wives of men stationed in the Philippines. The aircraft were PBYs, or patrol bomber (with the Y being the code assigned to the manufacturer). These were US Navy medium to heavy twin amphibious aircraft used for maritime patrol, water bombing, and search and rescue. In the 1930s, the Navy invested heavily in developing these long-range flying boats, which did not require runways, instead having the entire ocean to pick up speed to take flight.

An older colonel on the Rock told Sally it was Emperor Hirohito's birthday, so it was a good day to make a break for it and evacuate the last of the nurses. The colonel said it was certain that the Japanese would not be fighting that day, and sure enough, about noon all the enemy planes disappeared out of the sky. The women were anxious to get the evacuation over with, but the planes had to go through a safety check first. Each plane had a crew of seven, including the pilot and copilot, a navigator, a radio operator, a radar operator, and from one to four gunners. All equipment needed to be checked out. Add in a half dozen or more nurses in each plane, trying to get to safety, flying in 100-plus-degree heat pouring in the glass windows, and this was not a luxury ride.

"There were twenty-four of us who were evacuated from Corregidor that day," Sally later told friends. "We got on two different airplanes, PBYs, and that was where I ran into Col. Wood again. He oversaw the women on our plane, and I felt I could trust him."

Two planes holding Sally and the other nurses left Corregidor at midnight en route to Mindanao, the southernmost island of the Philippines, about 500 miles south of "the Rock." The plane needed to take on fuel at several points to make the four-thousand-mile trip to Australia. Sally could smell the fuel in the aircraft, and it made her stomach roil even more than the ride itself. The noise of the engines made it impossible to talk, and there weren't enough headphones for all of the nurses to listen to what the pilot was telling them. Sally just sat back and tried to will herself to stay calm; she was on the way to the safety of the shores of Australia.

They landed on Mindanao at about 4:45 in the morning, and the nurses had a leisurely day until they were to meet up again. The owners of the hotel there told the nurses they could all come to the hotel and get some rest, free of charge, before taking off again at dark. Sally was excited to sleep in a real bed with real sheets, even if it was for a few hours.

That afternoon, several nurses went to an open-air market where some local people were selling fresh fruits and vegetables, meat, nuts, and other foods. The women knew not to buy anything they couldn't eat on the spot because they didn't want to carry anything heavy back to the plane and risk weighing themselves and the plane down.

"At that market, I realized it was the first time I had been out in the daylight without being under gunfire since we fled from Manila!" Sally exclaimed. Was that less than four months ago? The time on Bataan had seemed like years instead of months. How could so many crazy things have happened in that short amount of time?

That night, the PBY crew and the women assembled at the landing dock. The first group got aboard and were towed out into the open water next to the landing. That plane took off in a huge spray of water. At the last minute, the crew of the second plane decided to take along some extra fuel, in case they had trouble finding another petrol stop along the route to Australia. Sally's group boarded that plane and prepared for takeoff. When the first plane was a safe distance out, the plane Sally was on started to taxi across the water away from the dock. As the plane prepared to taxi on the open water for takeoff, the bottom of the plane made a horrible screeching sound as it bumped over some huge boulders. Was that extra fuel the cause of the bottom-out? The fuselage now had a gaping hole in its underside. One of the nurses was wearing a terry cloth jacket. She got down on her knees and tried unsuccessfully to use her jacket to stem the flow of water. She quit trying when the water came up to her neck. The nurses all stood up in the plane, and the ankle-deep water in the cabin was rising fast. The pilot limped the plane back to the landing dock.

"Just think of it," Sally said to herself. "A matter of a few inches and we would have been saved."

But they didn't get saved. As soon as the plane pulled into the dock it had just left, the women began heaving their bags and themselves off that PBY plane as fast as they could. No one needed to explain to them that things were looking very grim. They didn't need a superior officer to give them orders to run like the wind. A dozen nurses stayed together, but they had trouble finding any place to hide.

First, they tried the hotel again. The proprietors seemed concerned about the nurses' plight earlier, so perhaps the owners would welcome them again. But they were reluctant to shelter the women now. Finally, after much hand gesturing because of the language barrier between English and Tagalog, it was agreed the proprietors would put the nurses up for the remainder of that night, if they left early in the morning. But Sally was so frightened, she didn't sleep at all, even in a real bed with real sheets.

That night, someone mentioned that maybe they might fix the plane, and they could still fly to safety.

"Fix it with what?" asked Sally. "Elmer's glue and army blankets and boards and whatever else they could find?"

On May 3rd, the sole navy nurse, a few more army nurses, and a small group of civilians were evacuated from

Corregidor aboard the submarine Spearfish. They made it all the way to the safety of the Australian shore.

The remaining nurses on Corregidor Island took a bed sheet, dated it, and each signed her name with a felt marker. The bed sheet was then hung on a wall in one of Malita's many tunnels. The nurses feared that they would all be killed by the enemy and their bodies would be disposed of, leaving their loved ones with no idea what had happened to them. They hoped the Japanese soldiers would not understand any English, so as not to destroy the bed sheet as well.

THE FALL OF CORREGIDOR

After the fall of Bataan, the Japanese had set their sights on Corregidor. When Corregidor fell to the Imperial forces under the command of General Masaharu Homma on May 6, 1942, the few remaining nurses were captured. On July 2nd, those nurses were transferred to the Santo Tomas Internment Camp in Manila.

The Abyss hissed again. That unseen, unexpected presence of pure evil that taunted many American and Filipino military staff was never more present than now in the dank, shadowy burrow of Malinta. Some feared they might tumble right down into the void. Would they all collide with their darker selves someday? Feelings like these were reminiscent of Halloween in the United States, where everywhere people wore gory costumes and pulled pranks to scare children. The same skin-tingling notion that fear was lurking everywhere was present in the tunnels under the rock of Corregidor. It was easy to believe

that something terrible would happen. They would all try not to think those thoughts, and they were kept very busy with new patients being brought in each day. They could also go "topside," up the ramp and out into the fresh air and sunshine. But could they find time in their already overfilled days? Before the enemy landed on Corregidor, outside it was nice, calm. They just had to watch and listen for incoming Japanese planes, shooting up the ground they stood on just before they rushed back into the Tunnel.

What was that evil feeling some had experienced, being kept underground in this awful war that most feared would not end well? What was that hissing noise?

PART V

PROMISE NOT TO CRY

Before the sun rose the morning of May 1, 1942, Sally and the other eleven nurses left the hotel on Mindanao. They were far from the dock and the disabled plane, with no sure plan for escape. They ran from place to place, trying to find a location where they could hide for a few hours until they needed to look for new, safe shelter. They stayed at a landing strip for three days. Most of the American and Filipino military and civilian aircraft had been destroyed or badly damaged, so an airstrip was a likely place to hide. But having twelve women cramped into a small airfield's office building was uncomfortable. And most of the women's personal belongings had been left on the plane when it began to take on water.

"I still have my musette bag," Sally said. The musette bag was like a courier's bag, flat to carry letters and small packages. Sally had managed to hang onto that bag, but she and most of the remaining nurses had lost their duffel bags by now. Sally also carried a small, precious cargo, wrapped in a silk handkerchief: $200 American dollars to buy airmail stamps for the letters, inside her musette bag, that doctors and other personnel gave her to mail when she got to safety.

The nurses finally found shelter in a private home, where they slept on the dining room floor for several nights. There were others there as well, including some male officers. Sally didn't get much sleep, and early one morning, she was certain she heard a plane. She saw two men in the next room that she recognized as Colonel Wood and a transportation officer. She got up and walked carefully between other nurses sleeping on the floor.

"Come outside," Sally said to the two men. She spoke softly because of the others sleeping nearby. When they were out the door, Sally said, "I hear a plane. Is that the one coming for us?"

The two men exchanged glances, and Colonel Wood said, "Well, Sally, we'll tell you something if you promise not to tell and not to cry."

Sally promised. The men told her the Japanese were coming very soon, May 6, 1942, and the American forces would formally surrender to the enemy. They would all—from the lowest clerical staff right up to higher-ranking officials—become prisoners of war.

Sally kept her promise. In fact, it never occurred to her to cry. The nurses had gone through hell and back, first in the jungle and then in the bowels of Corregidor Island. If they didn't cry then, they certainly weren't going to cry now. And there was no point in telling the other nurses what she now knew would happen. The other women would all find out very soon, probably that very day.

The announcement was soon made to all the Americans and Filipinos fighting the Japanese: they were to be taken captive that day. How could this have happened?

The first day of their captivity, the nurses and other American hospital staff were brought to Force Base Hospital #1 on the island of Mindanao. Sally's first escape attempt was aborted by the rocks in the water, and it looked now like there was again no chance of avoiding their fate. Force Base Hospital was staffed by one American doctor; the remainder of the staff were Filipino. There was a hospital barracks for the nurses, excellent accommodations, considering they were prisoners of war. The rooms were spacious, with many, if not most, amenities the nurses needed to be comfortable. The space was "billeted" (military personnel assigned to the living quarters of others, usually private homes, most often in times of war) from the currently assigned Filipino nursing staff, who had to be housed elsewhere to make room for the new captives. The American nurses were assigned two to a room, which was several steps up from a cot in a jungle full of wild creatures or stifling underground quarters on an island where staff rarely saw the light of day.

The nurses stayed in this posh arrangement until July 1942, when they were moved to Cagayan, a small town closer to the ocean, where it was hoped the Japanese could find a ship to transport their prisoners to Manila. When no ship appeared forthcoming, the American POWs were transported "in a dirty little boat" to Davao.

By this time, the Japanese had acquired some civilian missionary women whom the nurses were delighted to have along. "These women knew how to get along in these 'back woodsy' countries," Sally remembered later. The women missionaries were more than willing to share their hard-earned knowledge (as well as their faith) with the Americans. There was one male missionary who introduced himself as Mr. Downes. He had lived in Japan for twenty-two years, and he spoke the language fluently. Mr. Downes interpreted many early discussions between the Americans and their Japanese captors. Sally and the other nurses counted all this as a great blessing, a unique introduction to being a POW that was not shared by all who fell to that fate.

A SCAREDY CAT, A COWARD, OR JUST PLAIN NUTS

Sally did not think much of the transport that brought her and twenty-four other nurses to Davao. It was the third week of August, and the heat was oppressive. The boat—it could hardly be called a ship—needed to be brought into a dry dock and given a thorough scrubbing followed by a good coat of fresh paint. That was just for starters. Then, it could have used an engine tune-up so it didn't belch black, foul-smelling smoke constantly. In addition, the passenger "accommodations" were decidedly not five star, not even one star. The mattresses were crunchy, with fillings that felt like crushed-up crackers or some kind of animal feed. The sheets and blankets smelled clean, but they were of inferior quality, scratchy, and threadbare. Besides, there were crawling bugs and beetles and spiders climbing up the walls and open plumbing pipes. And that didn't even include all the complaints the nurses had about the food quality and quantity. The nurses were just beginning to learn how uncaring the Japanese soldiers were, at least the ones who were dealing with American and Filipino prisoners. And they were in no mood to take a ride in such a disgustingly grimy boat.

But the Japanese had told the group that they were to be repatriated to the United States soon, which sparked new hope for the nurses and others in their company. However, that ended up being a cruel joke. There were bigger ships waiting at Davao to take them back to Manila. And later, when some of the nurses tried to talk to the Japanese about their promise of sending them back to the USA, the soldiers just mocked them and said they did not understand what the nurses were saying. Fleeting hope was followed by more of the many cruel lies and disappointments the Americans would encounter at the hands of their captors.

They were on that boat for about four days. The group was given fresh water to drink but was not allowed to bathe or shower. The Japanese once again showed that they didn't seem to care at all. The feeling among the captives was that they could all die at sea, and the Japanese soldiers would simply look the other way.

Not to be completely defeated by her captors, Sally decided to have a bath one way or the other. She used her share of water for one day, and a friend gave her share to Sally too. The water fit in Sally's helmet, which she carefully carried to the hold of the boat and bathed with it in privacy. As she soaped up and wiped herself down, Sally vowed never to let feelings of despair take over her mind. Each of the nurses developed this approach, some with better results than others. But the nurses didn't get called "The Battling Belles of Bataan" for nothing. They were already widely recognized for their courage in the jungle. Now it was time to develop a plan, individually or together, to get themselves through this unfolding nightmare of captivity, one long day after long day.

After her improvised bath, Sally was feeling upbeat on her way up out of that hold. It was then that the dull roar she had heard while she was down there turned into a sharper moaning, like a person or an animal moving in for the kill. She shook her head and hurried up topside to breathe some fresh air. But she still heard the moaning that day and the next and the next. She never told anyone else because she thought they would mistake her for "a scaredy cat, a coward, or just plain nuts."

OH! YOU VERY SICK!

Everywhere they went, the nurses always considered themselves to be on duty—either formally or informally—anytime they were awake, and even if they themselves were not feeling well. Their consideration for others, Americans and Filipinos *and* their Japanese captors occasionally worked both ways, as Sally was about to find out.

A big ship arrived in Davao on the group's fourth day there. The ship was actually a nicely appointed cruiser with much-improved accommodations such as staterooms with balconies, two full-sized beds, bathrooms with showers inside each room, and colorful, good-quality bedding materials. There were even framed pictures on the walls in each stateroom. A deal was made between Japanese soldiers with guns and the ship's captain with no guns. Word came down that the ship was to take them to Manila. The twenty-nurse group was assigned to D Deck, but the ship wasn't full, so their cabins were very high out of the water. Sally and many others were still sick with malaria, dengue fever, and other gastrointestinal upsets. The ill nurses were concerned that the high deck would be swaying in open water, causing them to feel like vomiting. Whether because of the language barrier or another reason or reasons, the nurses could not get the Japanese to let them have staterooms on a lower deck. This most likely made passage unpleasant for the paying passengers who were given state rooms below the "actively ill" nurses.

For additional reasons that were not clear, the nurses' cabins could only be reached from the dock at Davao by climbing a rope ladder. Sally started up that ladder, with a malaria-induced fever of 103 degrees Fahrenheit, knowing if she looked down or up, she would get dizzy and throw up, or worse, fall off the ladder. They had to climb while holding a blanket that they had been given in which to bundle and carry the few possessions they still had. The blankets were tied shut, and by this point the nurses were lucky to have soap, a washcloth, and maybe a change of clothes rolled up in that blanket. Sally carried the blanket very carefully in front of her as she climbed, and she was careful to keep her gaze looking straight ahead toward the ship so she would not lose the contents of her stomach or the blanket roll or both.

Each of the nurses made it up the ladder and into their assigned cabins. Meals were served in a dining area cordoned off for the prisoners. Fortunately, there were interior stairs—not rope ladders—to reach the dining room. The first day on the water, Sally was lying in a deck chair with a high fever. Another nurse, Evelyn, took it upon herself to care for Sally, bringing her water so she could stay hydrated. Sally wasn't interested in food at this point, but Evelyn brought her small plates and encouraged her to eat to keep her strength up. The care Evelyn provided Sally was greatly appreciated, but the unspoken part of this arrangement was: what was awaiting these young women when they arrived at the prisoner-of-war camp?

One day, Sally and Evelyn were sitting out on the deck, and a Japanese medic stopped to talk to them. This was highly unusual because the Japanese soldiers just didn't interact with the prisoners, especially females. The two women were a little bit afraid of the medic. He took one look at Sally and said, "Oh! You very sick!" He spoke with a heavy accent, but he knew English. He had a thermometer and took Sally's temperature. He showed it to Sally, and it was still about 104 degrees. The medic gently touched Sally's forehead and quickly drew back his hand.

"Oh! You very sick! You HOT!"

Then he looked at Evelyn and said, "I got ice. You got ice cap?"

Evelyn did have an ice cap, which she showed him. The medic led the way, and they disappeared from view. He took her to the ship's kitchen and spoke to the head cook in Japanese. Then he switched to English so Evelyn would understand what was being said.

"I tell him," said the medic, "give her all the ice she needs for her sick friend and any others who have fever."

Evelyn was given ice to put on Sally's forehead, which helped keep her fever down. The medic appeared again a short time later and gave Sally two little black pills and a glass of water. Then he tenderly lifted Sally's head off the deck chair pillow so she could swallow the tiny pills. Sally didn't know what he was giving her, but she took them anyway. She thought about how humane this Japanese man, their captor, was to her, and she believed she could trust him.

There was an American woman on the ship who had lived in the Philippines all her life. She was not a prisoner; she just happened to be on the ship when the Japanese took control of it. She had a baby girl about six months old who couldn't crawl yet. The woman asked Sally if she could leave the baby on a blanket by Sally while the mother went to get her meals. Sally said that would be okay, although she doubted she could even sit up if the baby needed attention.

The first day, the little girl began to cry a few minutes after the mother left. Sally was helpless to quiet the child, but after a few minutes, the Japanese medic appeared. He bent over and patted the baby's back until she stopped crying. The medic backed away and watched the baby with tenderness in his eyes. When the baby began to cry again, the medic patted her back until she stopped. He tried this method several times, but each time, the little girl didn't stay quiet long. The medic finally picked the child up and cradled her in his arms. He held her body in his left hand and supported her head gently with his right hand. As he walked back and forth holding this complete stranger's baby, he began kissing her on her forehead. He walked and kissed her—so many times, Sally lost count—and finally the child fell into a deep, much-needed sleep. The medic put her back on the blanket, folding it around the baby. When he was sure she was sound asleep, the medic reached in his pocket and pulled out his wallet. He opened it and pulled out a small photograph of a baby and showed the photo to Sally.

"This my baby," he said. He pointed at the little child asleep on the blanket. "My baby boy!" he said, beaming. "This his picture eight years ago. I have not seen my baby since he that size."

Sally saw such tenderness in this man's eyes, she almost cried.

Another surprising incident involved a Japanese captor who came and asked the women to give him all their jewelry to take to his room for safekeeping. He seemed so nice and polite that most of the women who still had their jewelry gave him their necklaces, bracelets, rings, and earrings. He wrote everyone's name and possessions down and asked for help spelling the various gems and fine jewelry. As time passed and they came to their POW camp, many thought they would never see their jewelry again. But the Japanese man kept his word, and one day he showed up at the camp and was told the women were mostly working the morning shift at the hospital they had set up in the camp. They would all most likely be there caring for patients. The Japanese man asked for directions and off he went. He found every single woman who had given him jewelry and returned each piece to its rightful owner.

These were some of many humane acts that the nurses would see from the Japanese during their captivity. Kindness was rare, and life in a prisoner-of-war camp would prove to be very difficult. But light shone in the darkness when individuals—Japanese, American, Filipino—showed compassion for each other when the opportunity arose.

A MOTHER'S LOVE

It was a typical summer's day, as if anything was "typical." Since the fall of Bataan and Corregidor in early 1942, Sally's mother, Altie Blaine, usually suffered silently, trying to be stoic in her approach to life. Altie and her husband, William, had sold the farm and moved into a tiny clapboard house in the little village of Bible Grove. Then, William had died suddenly, probably of a heart attack. He was found lying inside a shed. There was no ambulance, so Altie called on neighbors and friends to help get William in somebody's truck and head for the nearest hospital. But Altie already knew that he was gone. She could tell, holding his head in her lap, that there was no movement, no rhythmic breathing, no reason to expect hope in this situation. Her husband and the father of her twelve children was gone.

Altie had lost one son in WWI, when he contracted a fever at boot camp. She had two other sons serving in the military, and she heard from them often enough to know they were safe. Altie tried not to think about her daughter, squalling around in a filthy POW camp. Altie's memories of just preparing a simple meal for her children and her husband were a comfort to her now. Often, she would send up a prayer or two for Sally's safety. And sometimes there were only dark thoughts that things would never change, that the world would be at war for a long time. Her little Ethel, who had chased those monarch butterflies one carefree summer was a long, long ways from home, and was in a very scary situation.

The mail came one day in late summer, so Altie wiped her hands and went to greet the carrier at the front door. The look the man had on his face was one of loss and deep sorrow. He handed Sally the letter; she knew it was bad news, but she was still hopeful about a prison swap, or something to rescue both men and women.

With shaking hands, Altie opened the letter with great care, but she dreaded reading it. Suddenly, a neighbor stood beside her. "Do you want me to read it, Altie?" the woman said.

Altie shook her head up and down.

The neighbor read the contents, which turned out to be a telegram. It read, "Mrs. Blaine, your daughter Ethel 'Sally' Blaine is confirmed to be alive and incarcerated at Santo Tomas University. You may write her there."

Altie could not hold back her tears. The neighbor surrounded her with a big hug, which surprised Altie. But she hugged her back and cried on the neighbor's shoulder. The neighbor continued to fill that terrible void a bit when she prayed for Altie and for Sally. At least Sally was alive, and she could receive letters! That brought hope, when her mother had thought, perhaps, she was already dead.

Santo Tomas Jesuit University/POW Camp (On next page)
Photo from the Ethel "Sally" Blaine Millett Collection

A CATHOLIC COLLEGE FOR THE PRISONERS

The University of Santo Tomas was the largest Catholic institution of higher learning in the Pacific Rim. The sprawling walled compound with grounds totaling 48 acres in size was easily commandeered by the Japanese invaders, since its most recent habitants for the last one hundred and fifty-seven years had been Jesuit and Dominican friars, pacifists by nature who possessed no weapons or locks against the outside world. The campus was well built and had been well cared for since the first part of the seventeenth century. When the nurses began to arrive, Santo Tomas was like a five-star hotel compared to some of the other Japanese POW camps in the Philippines, and it was a welcome change for those coming directly from the Bataan jungle hospitals and Corregidor Island's Malinta Tunnel, even though it meant the nurses were prisoners of the Japanese.

Santo Tomas also offered the recent jungle inhabitants a refreshing chance to see more normal scenes day to day. After Manila fell to the Japanese, the invaders set about rounding up most of the private citizens in the city who were suspected of favoring the United States. These citizens, many of whom were doctors, lawyers, and other professionals, as well as missionary families, were transported to Santo Tomas. This provided an opportunity for the POWs to have much-needed exposure to people from many walks of life and backgrounds. The nurses made numerous connections with these civilians.

"You're from Missouri? So am I…well, originally," said one woman who wore a baro't saya, a traditional ensemble consisting of a blouse (baro) and a skirt (saya) in beautifully patterned and elegantly draped fabric. "I've lived in the Philippines longer than I lived in Missouri."

"What part of Missouri are you from?" Sally asked.

"St. Louis," the woman replied. "And you?"

"Oh," said Sally, "you've never heard of the town I'm from!"

"Try me!" the woman said, clapping her hands. "I won a geography competition in high school!"

"Okay," said Sally with a twinkle in her eye. "My hometown is Bible Grove, Missouri."

"Oh," said the woman, "you got me there! What's the nearest big town?"

"Well, I guess Kirksville would be the closest. That's about thirty miles away."

"I know where *that* is," she answered.

And so it went. In spite of the hardships all the internees had and would experience, connections were made within the Santo Tomas compound, which made it feel more like a small town than a concentration camp.

The American and British "ex-pats"—short for "expatriates"—were people from a wide range of places and former lifestyles. Most made a conscious choice to live abroad; some had come as missionaries; some may not have been welcomed back in their home countries. Others came to the Philippines as tourists and just stayed put. Most had some monetary means to sustain this "bohemian" lifestyle. When the Japanese took civilians, those who had been employed were made to leave their jobs. There were children, teens, and young adults, with their parents or alone. Some of the boys and girls had been separated from their parents during the roundup and incarceration. Many parents were killed or captured and sent to different camps. Kids who found themselves alone at Santo Tomas showed remarkable resilience under the worst of conditions. Nurses, other medical staff, and the camp chaplains made sure these children connected with adults on whom they could rely. Adults took a special interest in these kids.

As the Santo Tomas civilian and military residents found themselves on the business end of the Japanese soldiers' rifles, they were quick to adapt to their new life. They wasted no time staking out a territory for themselves and their friends and families. They either claimed a space inside the massive buildings that made up the university, or if they were late arrivers, they built makeshift "shanties" in the courtyard, which was surrounded by the university buildings and a six-foot brick wall. This conglomeration of shelters in the courtyard became the preferred place many internees, including Sally, spent their spare time. Meals were cooked and shared using makeshift hibachis, liquor flowed, and someone always had a guitar or an ukulele, ready to start an impromptu song fest.

The "ex-pats" lived among the military prisoners and interacted with them on a daily basis. If this collection of prisoners of war behaved themselves, the Japanese largely left them alone, except for a mandatory roll call every night at 7:30.

Courtyard Shanties, Santo Tomas Internment Camp (STIC)
The creator of this specific photograph of the Santo Tomas Internment Camp is unknown. Photo found in the Ethel "Sally" Blaine Millett Collection.

The first nurses to arrive at Santo Tomas (not including Sally) talked among themselves, and it seemed in their best interest to make a deal with the Japanese. The arrangement was soon made that, if the nurses and the few expat and missionary doctors and others with medical training would agree to help staff the fully operational Catalena Hospital, treating American, Filipino, expat, other civilians, *and Japanese military personnel,* the

Japanese would leave the nurses alone. Catalina was one of the hospitals located within the larger complex of the University of Santo Tomas Hospital. Staffing schedules were created for the POW nurses, and the care of patients began soon after the POW camp was established. Sally said later that the Japanese steered clear of the women enlisted in the military, thinking the women must all be lesbians. In Japan, no women were ever allowed to serve in the military. The perception that women in uniform were "different" and even attained *officer status* may have been another reason the nurses were given a wide berth by their captors.

TELL HIM DON'S OKAY

When the small group of nurses from the cruise ship arrived in Manila, Sally recalled a gentleman who had told her, "Now, Sally, when you get to Santo Tomas, you look for Bert Holland and tell him Don's okay."

"How will I find Bert Holland?" Sally had asked him.

"Sally, everyone will know Bert Holland. Just ask for him."

Buses were waiting for the nurses when they disembarked the cruise ship commandeered by the Japanese soldiers. Someone was calling names from a list. Weak with fever, Sally stood close to the man with the list and listened for her name.

"Take this one to the hospital, Bert," the man said, pointing to Sally. Sally perked up.

"Bert? Bert Holland?" The man turned to her and smiled. "I'm Sally Blaine," she blurted out, "and Don's okay!"

Bert smiled and said, "How do you do, Sally Blaine? I'm Bert Holland, and that's very good news about Don!"

Holland was a delightful person, Sally decided right away. He was very personable and talked with Sally like he had known her all his life.

Since Sally was moving very slowly and appeared to be in rough shape, another man came up to her with a wheelchair.

"Do you need this?" the man asked.

"No," Sally said, "I can walk." But she could hardly move without help.

Sally was very ill, so Bert saw to it that she was taken to Catalina Hospital, where nurse POWs were already staffing the shifts.

When Sally was brought to Catalina Hospital, she slept for a long time. She took one look at that clean hospital bed, with the bright white sheets, and she felt peace for the first time since the bombing of Clark Field, which set this whole risky venture in motion. She could not have known, while her body fought to regain strength, that Catalina Hospital was the main medical facility at Santo Tomas Internment Camp, or STIC. One section was designated as a long-term care facility for many men who somehow survived the Bataan Death March in January of 1942. Sally knew many of the men who were made to march back to Manila after the fall of Bataan, but she had no idea which of them survived. As she slept, she did not know yet how many were now here at Santo Tomas, or how many had been shot to death along the way and left to die, their bodies serving as grim mile markers on the dirty road from Bataan to Manila.

When Sally became stronger and her mind was working overtime once again, she began to ask questions.

"Are you telling me that only a skeleton crew of Japanese soldiers are assigned to keep some 4000 internees in line?" she asked, astonished as hospital staff began to tell her about the internment camp in which they found themselves. "How is that possible?"

"It is possible," said an attending physician. "At times there are only 17 administrators and 8 guards. But they rule with an iron fist. In February before your group of nurses arrived, Sally, two young Englishmen and an Australian escaped from the compound. They were quickly recaptured and taken to a place just outside the compound. They were beaten and tortured, and finally forced to dig a large hole in the ground. Then they were forced to sit on the edge of the hole, and they were blindfolded. The Japanese guards executed them one by one and pushed their bodies into the hole."

"Oh, my *God!*" Sally exclaimed. "How horrible! Could the prisoners inside the compound hear the gunshots?"

"Yes," the doctor told her. "Worse than that, the internee leaders in the camp, including the room monitors where the escapees lived, were forced to watch the execution."

Sally wrung her hands in dismay. "Why would the Japanese be so cruel?" she exclaimed, close to tears.

"It was clearly a show of force, and yes, it was very cruel," the doctor said. "I can tell you, there have been no more escape attempts since then."

In the beginning of the Japanese occupation of the Philippines, most of the early civilian internees at Santo Tomas believed the United States would win the war with the Japanese quickly. They believed they would be liberated within a matter of weeks. But when they heard that Bataan fell to the Japanese, followed by the surrender of the American military on Corregidor Island, they adjusted their thinking to expect to stay captive for a while longer. After the nurses had made the pact with their Japanese captors, they set about doing a specific job every day, under less-than-ideal circumstances, just as they had when they were working in the jungle hospitals on the Bataan Peninsula. There were sixty-nine American nurses in Santo Tomas, including Sally, plus two dietitians and one physical therapist. All these personnel had served at the jungle hospitals on the Bataan Peninsula and knew each other well. A woman who worked for the Red Cross in Manila volunteered to be interred with the nurses and other hospital staff.

Everyone's duties were just like those of any other hospital, except most only worked four-hour shifts. Many of the women were so ill from malaria, dengue fever, and malnutrition, they could not be on their feet for a normal eight-hour shift. Those nurses who were able to work an eight-hour shift were assigned to the hospital housing the older men who had been severely injured on Bataan. It was a miracle that some of these men survived the "march"; some were missing limbs or had injuries that prevented them from walking on their own. But somehow, with the help of other soldiers and prayers to God, they ended up at Santo Tomas. The shadow of the loss of all those along the route from Bataan to Manila could be seen in the eyes of these survivors. There were three meals a day for these special patients and for the medical staff attending them.

Sally liked to work four-hour shifts in the morning because then they were given lunch. Sally tried to eat as much protein as she could, but meat and fish were given out sparingly. Many times, a whole day went by, and the internees received only two meals, morning and evening, consisting of rice and some variety of gruel—hardly edible. They learned to hold their noses and drink it fast so their stomachs would not growl so loudly.

ORGANIZATIONAL EXCELLENCE

Before the first few months had passed with prisoners being held at Santo Tomas, the Americans and the British had the place so organized, the Japanese didn't think about sending any of the prisoners to another POW camp. Santo Tomas was overcrowded, but the camp hummed with the precision of a well-oiled machine.

The Japanese selected a business executive from the ranks of new prisoners. This man was to create an "executive committee," sort of like a city council, and then begin the task of assigning duties. A British missionary who spoke fluent Japanese was chosen as an interpreter. A former Wall Street tycoon asked to be the head of the sanitation department. Some others chose their own positions, and some were simply assigned to a job. No one complained about the assignments, and soon, Santo Tomas was a "miniature city." The internees created a "town council," organized several committees, and staffed a police force (subject, of course, to the higher authority of their Japanese captors) to respond to conflicts and disputes among the POWs. Soon, the lives of Santo Tomas residents were rolling along in a neatly organized community.

A film made of the Santo Tomas Camp at the height of its occupation showed children running around playing, while their parents, dressed in their Sunday best, strolled around the plaza looking relaxed and even bored. Tremendous effort was made by the prisoners to don their best clothes and shoes, outfit their children similarly, and show themselves in public on Sunday afternoons and holidays.

In the spring of 1942, the Japanese allowed the remaining citizens of Manila to bring items to the captives and pass them through the gates of the compound. And in the first few weeks, certain wealthy Manila residents were allowed to drive into the compound to bring items directly to the internees. No doubt, many "gratuities" were passed from the Manila residents to the Japanese soldiers to facilitate these arrangements. The items brought in included food, paper goods, clothing, cooking staples such as sugar and flour, and money since an economic system was developing among those on the inside of the compound. Some expat prisoners brought considerable cash with them. Those who were not fortunate enough to have currency readily available, or who were caught off guard and rounded up quickly by the Japanese, suffered in the "new" economy of the camp. Even in a World War II POW camp, money talked.

The practice of bringing items to the prisoners was ended abruptly by the Japanese, with bamboo mats being attached to the fencing and the main gate being closed to outside traffic. The Japanese did still allow mail and packages addressed to prisoners after the parcels were thoroughly searched.

Before long, the daily census of the Santo Tomas Internment Camp rose to around 4,000 people. Soon, the governing committee began providing morning and evening meals to more than 1,000 captives who did not have food or money to buy it.

But even these broad-based accommodations would devolve into a hellhole of poor treatment of the prisoners by the Japanese. And as the war wore on and food became scarce, starvation and all its accompanying ailments ravaged all members of the Santo Tomas Internment Camp, leaving many captives with physical and emotional scars that would last a lifetime. Many male internees lost significant amounts of weight, often 30 to 50 pounds or more over the course of their internment. The women only fared slightly better.

Many people shared their unique talents or just pitched in to help wherever they could. A banker was greatly appreciated for washing mosquito nets (a necessity to get a good night's sleep, and more hygienic without dead insects lodged in the nets). He washed everyone's mosquito nets all day long and never seemed to mind. He wore a mosquito net himself while he worked. The insects would have attacked his whole body if not for the improvised suit he wore.

A shoe repair man set up shop in one of the shanties in the courtyard. Another man named Milton swept the corridors in the main building, and he would sweep right up to the nurses' rooms, which had only a curtain in the doorway. The man would never try to come in their rooms, and if he saw them in the hallway, he was always a perfect gentleman. That was one of the benefits of having the Americans take the helm in organizing a "little city" at Santo Tomas: the Americans policed themselves. The Japanese never had to intervene.

"These bed bugs are almost as bad as the mosquitos," Sally said to a friend as they changed their bed linens after washing them in boiling water. "They're like ants back home in Missouri."

Then there were the pigeons. The birds roosted just outside their third-floor window, leaving their droppings on the corrugated metal roof. When the sun was shining, the droppings dried and stuck like glue. In time, they began to smell. So, when they were not on duty, each nurse took her turn crawling out of a tiny window with a bucket of soapy water (it took three buckets to get the roof really clean). And then the birds were back.

It was Sally's day off, so she grabbed the bucket and started down the corridor to get water in the women's bathroom. Milton was sweeping the corridor, and he greeted Sally.

"What are you going to do with that bucket?" he asked.

"It's my day off, so it's my turn to wash the bird poop off the corrugated metal roof outside our room."

"Gimme that!" Milton said, and he started down the hall to the women's bathroom.

Too many women were using that bathroom, so he had to go all the way down the stairs to get water and soap to clean the rooftop. He repeated the process a total of three times and climbed through the small window three times to clean that roof. Sally considered Milton to be a good man, and he later married one of the nurses, the one who had been so kind to Sally when she was so sick on the ship on their trip to Manila. Sally also learned later that Milton was a wealthy business owner. His task of sweeping the floors in the women's billeted quarters was an example of the humility and kindness that flourished throughout the camp.

Meals were the same way. Because there were so many hungry people, the lines seemed impossible to endure. But everyone was polite and gentle with each other. Sally never remembered hearing a harsh word during any of those meals or in the lines to get fed. Some people didn't make it out of Santo Tomas, but the number of those lost would have been far greater without the compassion and caring of the prisoners who stuck together through the worst adversity of their lives.

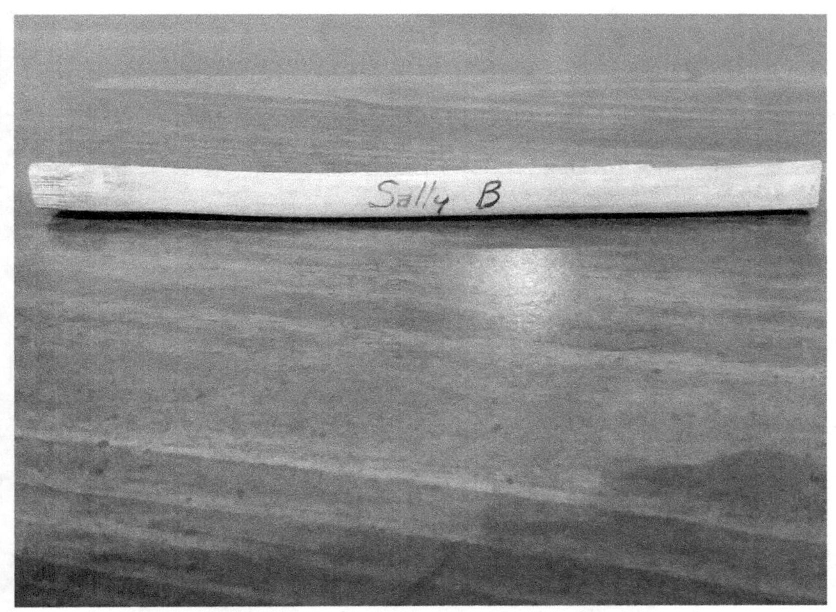

Clothespin Fashioned from a Bamboo Stick
Permission to use from the Sandra Phillips Wadley Collection

Although the prisoners were kind to each other, that trait often seemed lost on their Japanese captors. Those meals the internees so graciously accepted were often barely edible. The rice, the staple of all the meals they were given, was full of worms. The prisoners had to weigh their options: choke down wormy rice or spend the precious time they had to rest while sitting at a table picking out the worms.

In the morning, they had cracked wheat cooked as a "cereal." Sally liked the taste of the wheat, but some days it had more worms in it than the rice! At first, they were offered sugar for the "cereal," but soon that ran out. The internees had lots of ingenuity. Some would grind up coconut and mix it with the wheat, and then use the coconut milk to flavor it further. At first, those with money could buy coconuts from the vendors who were allowed to come in for short periods of time. But eventually, the vendors weren't allowed because the Japanese didn't trust them.

A SOURCE OF PROTEIN

The only meat they ever ate in the camp was cariboa (not the same as caribou), which was a domestic water buffalo brought to the Philippines from other parts of Asia. The animals were used as farm animals in times of peace. But when the war broke out, these beasts suffered a worse fate and were butchered to produce a tough and stringy meat. Usually, the meat was cooked and cut into tiny pieces. Then, small portions of the meat were mixed with a fatty broth, hardly enough to provide the daily protein that the prisoners needed to work even short shifts at the hospitals, or sweep floors, or any other of the many "volunteer" services the internees carried out each day.

Sally made friends easily, and one man became very dear to her, not in a romantic way but just as friends. He was an American, an expat named Dick who had lived in Manila for several years before the War. He had built a shanty in the courtyard, and he spent as much time as he could out there, except when he went to his job in the camp or came into the main building to sleep. His shanty was right next to the Japanese kitchen, so he kept a close watch for any food that was sitting out in the open.

"I don't care if Dick sometimes takes food from the Japanese," Sally said in a group of nurses. "Any of us would do it, any time we got the chance. They don't care about us, and they eat real well."

One night, Dick was at one of the communal sinks in the courtyard. A Japanese cook was standing next to him. The cook had a caribou liver, large enough to feed a few people for several meals. The cook was washing several things to prepare for the Japanese soldiers, and he must have lost track of how many items he had brought. He walked away without picking up the liver. Dick wasted no time picking up that caribou liver in its pan, but he didn't go into his shanty because it was so close to the Japanese kitchen. He practically ran with that liver to the other end of the courtyard, to a shanty his cousin and her husband had built.

"Look!" he said to his cousins. "A Japanese cook left this liver *right in the pan by the sink!*"

He showed them the liver, and they were astonished.

"You came to the right place," said the wife. "I brought some canning jars when I came to the camp. We can cut the liver up and can it, then hide it under our shanty in the hole we have dug."

The three prisoners set about cooking and canning the liver in some quart jars this resourceful cousin had on hand. Another friend of Sally's was there, and she ran quickly to the main building and found Sally getting ready for bed.

"Put your clothes back on!" she said to Sally. "We have to go to a shanty and help cook this caribou liver."

Sally figured the group could cook and can the caribou liver without her, and it was after the nighttime curfew when the Japanese made sure each prisoner was accounted for.

"I can't leave," Sally said. "There's a guard at the door downstairs."

"Oh," the friend said, "I have a white coat you can wear. I wear it when I work in the isolation hospital. I pass by the guard every night in my white coat, and he says nothing. Come with me and I'll give you a white coat and a pass to get out of curfew."

"I have a pass!" Sally said. "Don't use yours. You might need it later."

So, the two of them, in their white coats and with their passes, got right past the guard and practically ran to the shanty where Dick and his cousin and her husband were busy canning the liver. It took two hours to cook the liver over a small hibachi the cousin's husband had fashioned. The cousin revealed a hole under the bamboo mats on the floor of the shanty. They managed to get most of the canned jars into that hole, and they camouflaged it very well. What they couldn't get into the hole, they divided among themselves—except for Dick, who took none of it, for fear of being discovered. The American gave Sally several jars and a tote to carry them in. He asked a favor of her.

"Sally, I have some friends up on the third floor in the building where you have quarters too. My friends have never cooked for themselves because they always had domestic help," he said. "They don't know how to boil water, and they are starving. Give them two jars of the liver."

Sally agreed and took the tote with the jars of liver and headed to her quarters. Dick returned to his shanty empty-handed, and sure enough, the Japanese were looking for him. He let them search his hut, and then he "helped" them search all around that end of the camp. The Japanese didn't find the liver. After a while, Dick went back to his cousin's shanty and took several jars of liver in a large bag for himself.

Meanwhile, Sally walked back to the main building and delivered some of her jars of cooked liver to Dick's friends. Then she took the remaining jars up to the class-room-turned-nurses'-quarters she shared with several other women. She thought about what she would do with this meat that was such a precious commodity in the internment camp. She knew she deserved to take some of it. After all, her American friend had risked so much to take it and keep it hidden from the Japanese. She considered all the people she knew and eventually decided to give the meat to the woman doctor, a surgeon, who worked in the hospital Sally was assigned to. The doctor had children too. She found her in the main building that night.

"I want to give you a gift," Sally said to the doctor, "and you have to promise me you won't tell anyone where you got it."

"I promise," the doctor said. And Sally gave the doctor the liver.

"What's this?" the doctor asked.

"It's cariboa liver, all cooked and canned. Don't ask where it came from, " Sally said. "I want you and your children to have it." Sally touched the doctor's shoulder. "You do so much good for your patients, and your children need some real protein too."

Sally went back to her bed to try to sleep. She felt like a thief, but maybe the meat would help this doctor and her two children.

The next day, Sally saw the doctor at the hospital.

"Did you open the jars of caribou meat?" Sally asked her.

The doctor said, "I want to tell you about my decision about the liver. I share a space with three adults and my two children. If divided among them and me, that liver would not have made a difference to any of them to sustain them if we split it six ways. As the most valuable person in my group, I decided I should eat all the liver so I can take care of the people in the camp." She paused, then continued her explanation. "That way, I will be better able to focus on my work as a surgeon and thus help more than six people by far." The doctor saw that Sally was shocked at what she had told her. "I hope you understand my decision, Sally. It was such a generous gift from you."

"It was a gift to you," Sally said, obviously flustered. "You may do whatever you want with it."

Sally was very upset at first, thinking the doctor was being selfish. But the more she thought about the doctor's decision, the more she realized that this was the way the doctor "triaged" an impossible situation. She worked every day and helped many, many prisoners. Then she went back to the barracks and cared for her two little boys. And if she could get a boost from the liver, then that's what she thought was the best solution under the circumstances. Who was Sally to judge?

MORE FOOD PROCUREMENT

Another night, Dick the "liver thief" was sitting in his shanty enjoying a quiet evening. His neighbor came rushing in.

"Come with me, come with me!" he whispered. "The bodega is open where the sugar is!"

About fifteen feet from the first man's shanty and twenty feet from the Japanese kitchen, the lock on the door was broken and easily opened. The men grabbed some containers and rushed into the pantry, closing the door behind them. They filled the containers with sugar, covered their tracks, and rushed back to the shanty. They moved some furniture and the old rug on the floor and opened the hole dug in the shanty floor.

"Put the sugar in there. No one will find it!" the neighbor whispered.

"There's plenty of room. What a great hiding place," Dick whispered back.

The sugar was stashed inside, and the den was closed up and hidden again. Because the sugar had been stored in large bins, the Japanese never missed any of it.

The next morning, the man with the sugar in his hiding place found Sally.

"Come over when you can, and I'll tell you what I want you to do."

Sally went after her four-hour shift at the hospital.

"I need your help getting rid of the sugar we spilled on my shanty floor when we brought the loose containers in last night," the man said.

She and the man cleaned the floor of his shanty to get rid of all the loose sugar. Since the sugar was sealed up in airtight containers in the hidden hole, they used a lot of water to mop the floor free of every last granule. The Japanese never missed the sugar, and it lasted a long time.

As the war went on, eventually there was no cariboa and less and less of the minimum daily nutrition necessary for humans. By the end of World War II, the average weight loss for male prisoners at Santo Tomas was almost fifty-three pounds. Ten percent of the 390 prisoner deaths were attributed directly to starvation.

THE LOST GIRLS

The character Peter Pan debuted in J.M. Barrie's novel, *The Little White Bird* in 1902. The tale became a stage play entitled "Peter Pan, or The Boy Who Wouldn't Grow Up." The timeless classic is about a group of lads called the Lost Boys. Like Peter, these boys never grew up and they lived in a place called Neverland. A memorable scene finds Peter and the Lost Boys pretending to have a grand feast, with lots of delicious food. In reality, they have absolutely nothing to eat. Such is the childlike, mystical world of Neverland, where pretending often must be substituted for the real thing.

The nurses interned at Santo Tomas might have been called "The Lost Girls" when it came to their thoughts about food. Idle time often found them remembering their favorite foods, recipes, ingredients, traditions, and memories of their homes "stateside" which they longed for every day in the POW camp.

"What's your favorite pie?" one nurse would ask.

"Peach!" "Pecan!" "Cherry!" "No, apple all the way! With crumble topping and caramel sauce and a wedge of sharp cheddar cheese on the side of the plate!"

"And all the women in my family make their pie crust with lard."

"Oh, no, my family started using Crisco, the solid vegetable oil. It's much better for you, not as fattening as lard."

"Oh, YUK!" came a chorus of replies. "It's lard *or* NOTHING in our house!"

The discussion continued.

"Did your mother can meat?"

"Oh, yes, chicken, beef, pork, venison, and anything the men could shoot. She'd can anything at all for us to eat in the winter."

"My mother canned pork sausage formed into meatballs," Sally said. "Nothing smells better in the middle of the winter than when my mother pops open a couple of gallon jars of her sausage balls. The whole family comes running."

"I'd give anything to sit down at my family's table at Thanksgiving or Christmas and feast on all those wonderful dishes: turkey and goose cooked crisp and brown, sage stuffing inside the birds, and mounds and mounds of fresh mashed potatoes with lots of butter," Sally continued. "And the *breads!* Oh, my goodness! The Blaines all love our bread! And don't get me started on the fresh canned vegetables and fruit jellies and jams and..."

"Oooooh, I remember when our mother discovered Jell-O, and all the recipes you can make from *that*! The flavors and different tastes were endless!"

"What's your favorite Jell-O recipe?" "That sounds delicious..." "Do you remember how to make it? Can you write it down for me? Please try to remember!"

And so it went. Even though none of the women would have any of the ingredients, including Jell-O, to make the dishes they talked about, they still entertained themselves for hours thinking about real food. They loved talking about remembered recipes and ways to cook various dishes, about shared food and celebrations with food, and family members lovingly making food. All of this came at a time when, in reality, they ate wormy gruel, were weakened in body by malaria and dysentery, but were sustained by their indescribable caring and dedication to their bond as prisoners of war day after day after day.

They could oManila residents were nly dream of the wonderful feasts they hoped to have again one day with their loved ones. And they were kept going by the needs of their precious charges in the hospital and long-term care facility. Nothing was more important than their patients.

When the remaining expats and other residents of Manila were still allowed to visit the Santo Tomas compound, one inexpensive item they brought were vegetable seeds. Such a small gift could yield a huge crop of vegetables under the right conditions. But no matter how much experience the prisoners might have had raising garden vegetables, the conditions at Santo Tomas weren't always ideal for vegetable gardening. To begin with, it was hot in the Philippines, so crops took a lot of water to grow. And water was rationed among prisoners (though the Japanese captors seemed to have plenty). Too often, seedlings would just dry up before they had a chance to grow and produce food. But the nurses still tried to grow what they could, and since they could plant year round. they learned the tricks needed to grow some basic vegetables.

OVER THE FENCE DELIVERY

The Japanese decided somewhere along the line that they didn't mind the "Over the Fence Delivery" program because they benefited from it too. They particularly liked fountain pens and wristwatches, and they could be seen bartering for these items and more, right alongside the prisoners. All kinds of jewelry, too, made the Japanese sit up and take notice, and they loved to barter for whiskey. When the Japanese were bartering, that meant they were walking away from their posts and not thinking about what the Americans and others were getting away with. The longer they bartered with the people on the other side of the fence, the more the prisoners were able to keep bartering themselves. Cooking staples like flour, whole grains, and yeast for bread making; butter; and salt and pepper were popular, plus cooking utensils and bowls and plates—anything to make a meal a little more appetizing. Manila residents brought treats like chocolate and hard candy, asking little to nothing in exchange. The people really wanted to help the internees out. They had no loyalty to those occupying their homeland, and many residents were already friends with the ex-pats who now lived among the military prisoners at Santo Tomas.

But if the guards actually *saw* the prisoners participating in the "Over The Fence Delivery" program, they were quick to act. Great show and fanfare took place as the prisoners in question would be ceremoniously thrown into their "Prison Within A Prison," with much puffing of chests and bragging in Japanese about how they had apprehended these sneaky prisoners, now accused of doing the exact same thing the soldiers were doing ten minutes ago. The "prisoners" going to this internal "prison" were not particularly worried about the treatment they might receive. They were only given rice and water, but they had endured the fate of insufficient food most of the time anyway. And the guards were outnumbered by the internees by hundreds of prisoners to Japanese soldiers, so there wasn't a tight-knit security force staffing the little prison. When the guards went back to their official post, most of the detainees just opened the gate of the jail and walked out.

Another strange practice developed between the residents of Manila and the Japanese guarding Santo Tomas. Because war had been declared and the Japanese had "captured" the entire Philippine Islands, technically anybody who was not part of the invasion could be picked up and taken to Santo Tomas or another POW camp for no reason. The Japanese began paying visits to various people living in Manila who might "enhance" the already burgeoning population of the camp. A couple of soldiers would come unannounced and bang on the doors of city residents.

"Wait here for transportation," the Japanese would tell them, often visiting them before breakfast. "We will take you sometime today, and you will be placed at Santo Tomas. Bring enough clothes and food to last you for three days."

After the soldiers left, the people would begin to pack up things they wanted to take with them when they were taken to the POW camp. And then they would wait. And wait. And wait. Many times, the Japanese never came back. It was as if they had forgotten all about the threat they had made to take these residents into custody.

Others were picked up later, and as instructed, they brought enough clothing, food, and supplies for just three days. They thought they would be let go after three days, or that they might be moved. But the ones who were picked up by Japanese soldiers and brought to Santo Tomas were there three *years*, not three days. No one questioned this strange practice, and none of those "captured" in this way were ever released early or sent to other camps.

NEW LIFE

For four generations, Hollywood has been attempting to interject romance into wartime motion pictures. After the 1915 American film "The Birth of a Nation" included a subplot of a love affair, movie producers were off to the races trying to gain more viewership by interjecting passion and ardor into every possible war scenario. Early movie producers would have been thrilled to know that Santo Tomas Internment Camp saw seventy-five babies born between 1942 and 1945. These births occurred despite the challenging conditions and strict regulations imposed by the Japanese soldiers. There were 45 births in the first year, with the annual number down to 2 births in 1945. Obviously, many couples were already expecting before they were taken to the camp. Extreme rationing of prisoner food may have caused couples to limit their intimacy as time went on. It's hard to think about romance and passion when your stomach growls constantly.

There is nothing in the world that more reliably brings joy and hope than the birth of a new baby. Catalina Hospital, where the army POW nurses worked, had a labor and delivery department. The larger University of Santo Tomas Hospital, which housed Catalina, had a more complex labor and delivery department capable of handling low- and high-risk deliveries. Santo Tomas Hospital also operated neonatal intensive care units (NICUs) to serve premature babies and babies born with life-threatening issues. It goes without saying that these babies, born to mothers who had already been deprived of a complete and nutritious diet, were not in the best condition when delivery occurred. Since infant formula was not readily available, and cow's or goat's milk was difficult to get, the mothers had to breastfeed. There simply were no other good options. And the lack of proper nutrition and hospital equipment made breastfeeding challenging for mothers and babies.

The majority of the new mothers were American, followed by a small number of Filipino, British, New Zealander, and others. Efforts were made to provide extra food for mothers and infants. Although rationing was still very strict, mothers and babies were given more food when it was available. Sympathetic Filipinos and other internees would barter for extra food within the camp or "through the fence." This was risky, but the importance of better food for these nursing mothers and their growing babies was a top priority for many in the camp. The resilience of these POW mothers and their children is astounding. And the fact that the earliest children born in the camp were over three years old when the war ended speaks volumes about the strength and grit of the parents of these wartime toddlers. This stage of a child's life is marked by rapid growth and development, including learning to walk, talk, and explore their surroundings (including food!) they find themselves in. It should be an exciting time for both the children and their parents. Imagine trying to respond to all a toddler's needs in a prisoner-of-war camp!

CHRISTMAS AT SANTO TOMAS

In spite of the dismal circumstances in the internment camp, at Christmastime, the prisoners sought once again to make life seem as normal as possible, especially for the children.

The first year the prison camp was in operation, 1942, there was quite a celebration. The prisoners created a "Santa's Workshop," making toys from any materials available: scraps of wood, metal, bamboo a little left over paint. Used toys were donated and the internees refurbished as many as they could. The prisoners were still allowed to have visitors from the community, and kindhearted friends and total strangers showed up with more gifts for children and adults, as well as food. Roasted turkey and pork and also ice cream were on the menu that first year. The children all gathered around a large, decorated Christmas tree, and Santa wore a used costume donated from outside the camp. The children squealed and laughed with glee when Santa arrived and passed out presents with their names on them.

The nurses had similar celebrations among themselves, with the women making gifts or getting some rare commodity like chocolate or instant coffee or tea from outside the compound. They also exchanged handmade presents constructed from limited materials. Jewelry, small art objects, and whatever they could put together served as presents among themselves. Handwritten notes were popular all year long, expressing thanks for the support and care of the other nurses. The small gifts were a tribute to the resourcefulness of the nurses in captivity. They continued to form strong ties for their entire incarceration.

By 1943, supplies in the entire camp were dwindling, but the internees still tried hard to celebrate Christmas. Acts of kindness were a gift that cost nothing and needed no materials except a kind heart and a motivation to show each other how much they cared. Details of holidays during those years were not well documented, but the general spirit of the camp was important, and most prisoners tried their best to show the Christmas spirit.

Conditions had deteriorated significantly by Christmas 1944. Food and supplies were running crucially low. The determination of the prisoners to keep the Christmas holiday alive was admirable. As time went on, little was documented of the celebrations. At least some of the prisoners later reported the remembrance of the holiday, showing the indomitable spirit of the prisoners.

THAT'S ENTERTAINMENT!

"**G**ood morning, Santo Tomas!" a deep male voice boomed over a cobbled-together camp loudspeaker system. "It's gonna be another Muggy Monday here in the City of Captivity, right inside downtown Manila. First up this morning is a report on how the Emperor of Japan has grossly underestimated the power of the Military Might that is the Armed Forces of the U-S-of-A! Let's hear it for our men and women on the front lines of this war, and let's celebrate how they are taking down the puny little Japanese Military as we speak! Take THAT, Emperor Hirohito and your bloodthirsty generals!" (Shouts, whistles, and clapping could be heard throughout the Santo Tomas compound.)

"In other news," the voice continued, "some of our Partying Prisoners have found where the monks at Santo Tomas stored their Mogan David communion wine. And one short public service announcement: there will be a wine-and-rice tasting party—sorry, no cheese to be had—at 1700 hours in the last shanty in the southeast corner of the courtyard. Remember everyone, it's 1700 hours some-where, all day and all night! Celebrate responsibly and please arrange your ride home before you indulge."

Clarence Alton Beliel, commonly known as Don Bell, was an American radio broadcaster best known for his work in the Philippines in the years before World War II. Bell joined the Marines at a young age, wanting to serve overseas with the goal of becoming a foreign correspondent. He served as a Marine in China for six years, after which he worked for an American-owned, English-language daily newspaper in Shanghai. When the paper acquired a radio station, Bell added broadcasting to his journalistic pursuits. With the Japanese invasion of China in 1937, Bell fled to Manila. There, he served as a foreign correspondent for NBC and as a program coordinator for British, Czech, and French news organizations. Bell also worked for Radio Manila, and his broadcasts were one of the main sources of news for the English-speaking population in the Far East.

When the Japanese invasion of the Philippines appeared imminent, Bell was enlisted by the Philippine government and General MacArthur's headquarters to help maintain morale by continuing to broadcast hourly. He continued his broadcasts until the radio transmitters had to be destroyed to prevent them from falling into the hands of the enemy.

At the Japanese invasion of the Philippines, Bell dropped his radio name and assumed his legal name of Clarence Beliel. Bell arranged to be taken into custody by the Japanese while he was working at a Manila department store. The deception was maintained by all who knew him as Don Bell. To have revealed that he was the person who had broadcast many anti-Japanese sentiments would have led to dire consequences for the journalist. Bell was interned, together with his wife, Lilia, and two sons, Clarence and Richard, at Santo Tomas University in Manila. Shortly after his arrival, he was up and running again—not exactly the kind of broadcasting he was used to, but a few loudspeakers and some slapdash wiring did the trick. The Japanese never shut him down. They thought he was just some amateur and they could not understand one word he was saying.

Another professional in the field of journalism was Carl Mydans, who was a photojournalist for *Life Magazine* for four decades. Mydans produced stories about Hollywood celebrities, Texas cattle roundups, and the Jim Crow era in the Deep South. His most important assignment was as a war photographer. He turned his camera to the perspective of an infantryman as the best way of showing what war felt like. In January 1942, he and his wife, Shelley, then a *Life* researcher-reporter, were taken prisoner by invading Japanese forces in Manila; they spent almost two years in captivity at Santo Tomas before being released in a prisoner exchange. While he was interned there, Mydans photographed many prisoners and captors and illustrated events both tragic and poignant. His ability to tell a story through a single face would distinguish his career. One of his most widely reproduced war pictures shows Mydans's friend, General Douglas MacArthur, wading ashore on Luzon, Philippines, in October 1944, illuminating the fulfillment of his 1942 pledge to return to the Philippines.

While Don Bell kept the spirits up over the airwaves, and Carl Mydans honed his legendary photography skills on the prisoners and their captors, others contributed to the merriment at Santo Tomas as well. There was a gymnasium, a baseball league, a little league for children, musical programs, and a number of movies shown from time to time.

"You know I had to be pretty sick to miss a movie," Sally said later.

"I missed that movie because I was the first person operated on as an emergency surgery in our new operating room," she continued. "The Japanese finally allowed us to equip the surgery room with wonderful German instruments. You know everything the Germans make is good," she said.

Sally was impressed with how heavy the German-made surgical tools were, unlike American-made instruments, which were flimsy in comparison. When Sally had rotated into the surgery department at Santo Tomas, she saw firsthand how nice the new tools were. Sally felt she was in good hands

"An American surgeon using German instruments performed surgery on another American in a Japanese prison camp" was the way she described it.

Also set up early in the period of captivity were the schools and structured activities for some 400 children. From the very beginning, the leaders of the camp government always considered the children in all their planning. Since the goal of the camp "government" was to preserve, mirror, and reinforce Western culture, values, and individual worth as they navigated Japanese control of the camp, it was deemed important to give the children structure as well as careful mentoring in an uncertain environment. The morale of the children was important to monitor, since the children looked to their parents for assurance that things would one day be back to normal. In many ways, the children enjoyed a freedom their parents did not share, since the adults knew exactly what their lives were worth to the Japanese. For the children, being in the camp was a new experience, with new friends and a new format for school, plus plenty of time to explore the buildings and grounds at Santo Tomas. The only buildings off limits to the children were the ones occupied by the Japanese guards. Even the guards turned a blind eye to the children roaming free in the compound. Perhaps the Japanese were reminded of their own children back home.

The Japanese allowed American doctors living in the Philippines to come into Santo Tomas to help because of the large number of internees and the small number of captive doctors. These full-time residents of the Philippines from the US most likely had to demonstrate that they were not spies or other undercover workers for the

US's or Philippines's causes. But even the Japanese got sick and needed surgery from time to time, and they weren't going to allow their health to be in jeopardy because of a lack of doctors. Even the commander of the Japanese forces guarding Santo Tomas got sick.

"It wasn't serious," Sally said. "Just diarrhea, I think. He came into the camp hospital and was treated by one of the American missionary doctors. The commandant was feeling well the last night he spent there. The doctor said, 'I think by morning you ought to be well enough to go. But I'd rather see you in the morning before you go back to work.' The next day, the Japanese officer got up very early and dressed himself. He sat on his bed, had his sword by his side, and waited for the American missionary doctor—his prisoner—to give him permission to go back to duty. The Japanese had great respect for authority, especially medical doctors."

THE CAVALRY IS (MAYBE) COMING

As early as August 1944, the prisoners at Santo Tomas were hearing about American military action in the Philippines. Was the long wait for the arrival of the cavalry about to end? A few hidden radios were maintained by internees, and the reports were coming in rapidly. On September 21, the Americans conducted the first air raid on Manila. The Philippine Island of Leyte, on the south end of the island nation, was invaded by American forces on October 20, 1944, and the US advanced on Japanese forces on neighboring islands.

Soon, American bombers led daily assaults on Manila.

In late 1944, it began to be clear that the Japanese captors were nervous. On December 23, the guards arrested three of the leaders of the internees. Word was the Japanese thought this camp leaders had somehow been in contact with Filipino soldiers and guerrilla forces and were operating as spies. On January 5, 1945, the three men were taken outside the camp and beheaded. One of the men was named Larson, but there were two Larsons in the camp, and the guards got the wrong one. It all happened so fast, but eventually the internees figured out what happened—

that the wrong Larson was executed. None of the internees knew of the men's exact fate until their bodies were later found lying where they had been executed.

When the men were shot to death, the Abyss roared so loudly, it rang in the ears of every internee at Santo Tomas for weeks. The unspeakable evil the Japanese were capable of was astounding to all the prisoners.

The guards inspected the internees' rooms throughout the years they were at Santo Tomas. But the inspections increased during January 1945.

"I never had a real fear of the Japanese harming me," Sally said. "I know it was because of that one guy, the medic, on the boat who was so good to me."

In one of the last room searches, Sally remembered being nervous.

"I was a little uneasy because I had money in a cigar box, American money, and I had some letters." And she was afraid the Japanese would take the money and destroy the letters.

"They really were letters my mother had sent to me, and they were in the cigar box." The money was underneath the letters.

The guard stood in front of her with his gun pointed at her. Neither of them could understand each other, but Sally pushed the cigar box in front of the guard.

"Here," she said, "Letters from home! Letters from home!"

The guard drew closer and looked straight at Sally.

"I showed him what I had, the cigar box and some letters. But he didn't take anything from me. If I'd tried to take it back or hide it behind me, he would have reached for it, of course. So I outfoxed him."

Two weeks later, suddenly there were no guards in the camp at all for about forty-eight hours. The Japanese just walked out of the camp, a few at a time, until they were all gone. None of the internees tried to leave the camp because they thought it might be a trap. The prisoners were still reeling from the executions two weeks prior. Everyone in camp stayed put, business as usual. The nurses and doctors went to their assignments at the hospital, the children were sent to school, and everyone who had a job to do made sure it got done.

Then, two days later, the Japanese guards returned to the camp the same way they left: a few at a time, alone or together, back to their duty stations with their weapons ready to fire upon any prisoners who caused trouble.

But it was a sign that things were becoming "different."

Then, the Japanese made all the internees sign a paper agreeing that they would do no harm to the Japanese army.

"What would you do?" Sally said afterward. "They had the guns, the sabers, the swords. What would you do? We signed. And not a one of us felt like we were signing away anything because not a one of us would not have broken that pact," Sally said. "I stole from the Japanese," she added. "We all did."

The internees didn't owe the guards any favors. They had mostly behaved themselves and gone about their business of keeping the camp running the best they could. They signed the papers, but it meant nothing. "And I would do it again—steal, sign the paper, anything. Everyone felt the same way. You didn't care."

Around the first of February 1945, a group of boys were playing soccer when they heard the unmistakable sound of American fighter planes overhead. Everyone knew the distinctive sound of the four Wright R-1820-97 Cyclone radial engines, each producing 1,200 horsepower. It was not hard to recognize the Boeing B-17 Flying Fortress compared to the Japanese Mitsubishi counterparts.

"Look!" shouted one boy. "It's American planes! They're coming to rescue us!"

"How they gonna do that?" said another. "They're way up there in the sky and there's no landing strip anyplace nearby!"

The planes were directly overhead now, and the boys saw an arm come out of a cockpit window. Then they saw a dark object falling from the sky.

"What is THAT?" the first boy said. "It looks like a pencil box."

"Or a tobacco case," said a third boy.

By now some adult men began to run toward the group of boys. When the object fell to the ground and bounced a couple of times, several of the bystanders backed away.

"What if it's a bomb?" someone said.

"Who's going to drop a bomb from an American plane into a POW camp?" said one of the men.

"Somebody pretty stupid, that's who!" shouted one of the boys.

A man standing among them walked over and picked the item up.

"Why, it's only a goggles case...and look what's inside?" he said calmly. "The note says, 'Roll out the barrel. There'll be a hot time in the old town tonight!'"

Don Bell found recordings of those two songs and played them on his crackly loudspeaker, over and over and over again until the inmates were stuffing their ears with cotton. But Don wouldn't give up. His mission was to make life easier for the internees, with laughter, and music, and fun. The liberation appeared imminent, and Don wanted to create an atmosphere of celebration in the entire camp.

The American planes repeated their flights over Santo Tomas. Each time a note was dropped to the ground, the crowd grew, and a similar message attached to a heavy object was intended for the prisoners. Something was up. Everyone knew it, but they were still a bit skeptical. Could it really be true? Were the Americans really winning the war with Japan? Could their liberation be imminent? Would they all be released, or would more be killed even as the Japanese lost control—especially as the Japanese lost control? This enemy had been known to kill all prisoners, civilians, even children, if they had a mind to. And no one wanted to encourage that wrath by rebelling or trying to escape from the camp.

THE CAVALRY IS (REALLY) COMING

February 3ʳᵈ was just an ordinary day
at Santo Tomas POW camp.

The efficiently organized prisoners on the morning shifts of their various assignments arose, dressed, perhaps ate a less-than-satisfying breakfast of wormy rice cereal, and proceeded to their jobs. The sanitation crew removed trash and spruced up the outside of the buildings around the compound, reminding the shanty dwellers to be sure to pick up after themselves, as was the agreement when the shanties began to pop up all over the courtyards. At the hospital, scheduled surgeries were conducted with the high-quality surgical instruments that had been donated to the prison hospital. Patients on the medical wards were fed, washed up, and received the daily testing of their vital signs. Blood was drawn and sent to the lab for results to help monitor patients' treatment plans. Patients were walked around the ward by orderlies to help build strength and balance; some were even taken outside if the day wasn't too hot. Nurses, doctors, and orderlies worked side by side and took their breaks in the same break room. A common goal to "just keep plugging along" led to a palpable sense that they were all equal, all there for the same purpose: to *survive,* and to help others survive. More than once, the nurses remembered their beloved patient and friend, Angelito, and how he would tell the nurses they were *the embodiment of hope* for all the prisoners. The nurses never felt they deserved the honor; they only wanted to give their patients the very best care they could under the circumstances.

Night fell, and the day shift prepared for bed, in sweltering rooms without fans. The windows could not be left open for a little breeze because of the mosquitoes. The bed nets were scarce, and most had tears, and the mosquitoes would find their way through the tiniest hole, threatening to infect everyone nearby with deadly diseases. The night shift had gone to work a few hours earlier, and the business of the village of Santo Tomas went on as usual.

Unbeknownst to the internees, a small contingent of American forces was advancing toward Santo Tomas to liberate the POWs. Efforts throughout the Philippines were being forged to release all internees. It was commonly believed the Japanese would massacre all prisoners, military and civilian, rather than give them up to the enemy. As hope for the liberation kept Santo Tomas spirits cautiously high, everyone was weary to the bone of the whole situation. For many, death seemed inevitable, and it didn't make much difference when the Grim Reaper came calling: before or after some type of intervention.

Then, on February 3 and 4, the prisoners heard tanks, grenades, and rifle fire near the gates of Santo Tomas.

LIBERATION!

On February 5, 1945, 1,127 days since the first internees were brought to Santo Tomas, the 44th Tank Battalion crashed through the gates of the compound at 8:40 p.m. The first two tanks to enter the camp had their names emblazoned on each side: "Battlin' Basic" and "Georgia Peach." Unfortunately for the internees, although they were liberated, the Battle of Manila raged all around them, and the campus was caught in the crossfire of shelling. Some internees were hit with shrapnel in the clash. Injured soldiers, there to liberate the captives, lay on the same ground where the children had played soccer just yesterday.

Liberation! Front of Main Building at Santo Tomas. Sally's Room Was #41, Second Floor Right of Flag

The photograph was taken by Carl Mydans, a photographer for Life magazine. Photo found in the Ethel "Sally" Blaine Millett Collection.

There is a photograph of a number of the Santo Tomas Hospital nurses, smiling, with their hair all tied up with kerchiefs, sitting in the back of a truck in front of the main building at the POW compound. It's an easy assumption to believe that the soldiers who drove those tanks *into* Santo Tomas jumped out of the truck and, in typical Hollywood fashion, swept the nurses into their arms and drove back out of the compound with the women in tow. That version is close to how Hollywood rewrote the script as postwar movies abounded. But nothing could have been further from the truth.

Unsurprisingly, a small skirmish ensued when the first American tank broke through the gate to the Santo Tomas camp without warning. The Japanese had not heard of a surrender, and they were very afraid of what their commanding officers might do to them if they did not defend their post and keep their prisoners in line until their very last breath on this earth. No nurses got swept up and taken anywhere by anyone. In the midst of a new and much closer battle, the nurses went back to work at the hospital to take care of their current patients and several new ones arriving during the skirmish between the Japanese guards and the American troops.

The doctors and nurses seamlessly rededicated themselves to their pledge to respond to injuries and illnesses among the enemy troops as well. Catalina Hospital at Santo Tomas Internment Camp was quite a scene, with soldiers from both sides of the battle being treated side by side in the emergency rooms and surgery bays.

Liberation! American Internees and G.I.s at Santo Tomas Internment Camp February 3, 1945

Photographer unknown. Photo found in the Ethel "Sally" Blaine Millett Collection.

As the Americans appeared to clearly have the upper hand, the Japanese soldiers moved to the three-story Education Building, which had served as their enemy headquarters for the duration of the internment in the Jesuit compound. They took about 200 internees as hostages, including leader Earl Carrol and interpreter Ernest Stanley. Carrol and Stanley were forced to accompany some Japanese to meet with Americans to negotiate a safe passage for the Japanese out of Santo Tomas. In exchange, the Japanese would release their 200 hostages.

During an initial meeting between the Americans, Filipinos, and Japanese, a Japanese officer named Abiko reached into a pouch on his back, apparently for a hand grenade, and an American soldier shot and wounded him.

Abiko was especially hated by the internees. He was carried away by a mob of enraged prisoners, who kicked him and slashed him with knives. Eventually, he was taken to the hospital. They laid Abiko in a bed that had been occupied by a woman who got up to use the toilet. When she came back and saw a Japanese soldier in her bed, she pushed him off onto the floor and reclaimed her spot. Abiko lay on the floor for several hours before he succumbed to his injuries and died.

Liberation of Santo Tomas Internment Camp February 3, 1945
The photograph was taken by Inez McDonald, a nurse who was interned at the Santo Tomas Internment Camp during World War II. Photo found in the Ethel "Sally" Blaine Millett Collection.

It was bedlam in the hospital. People were running in and out and all around, attending to the wounded. All shifts were suspended, and any staff who were awake and breathing were in the hospital at their posts.

Another nurse said to Sally, "They took Abiko to this room over here. He's dead. Let's go look at him."

Sally didn't want to go, but she followed the other nurse to have a look. Sally felt sick to her stomach. She took no joy in seeing this dead man who had been one of the Japanese leaders, who had not treated his prisoners well at all. Sally thought it was just depressing to see this dead man. The whole mess was so dismal, she couldn't even process that now they would be free. She couldn't imagine what that would feel like.

She turned and left the room where Abiko's body lay, and she went back to work at Catalina Hospital. Because, after all, all she ever wanted to be was a nurse, and all she ever set out to do was care for the patients in her charge.

At the end of the day, the Angels of Bataan didn't want to be thought of as angels or remembered as heroes. All they ever wanted to be was just nurses.

Just nurses.

Lieut. Ethel L. Blaine (center) of Greensburg, Mo., one of the Army nurses held captive by the Japs after Corregidor fell, was greeted by her brother, Col. M. D. Blaine (left) of Washington, D.C., and her sister, Mrs. Jessie Crowder of Richmond, when she arrived here today. These pictures were taken at Hamilton Field.—A.P. Wirephotos.

Col. Mayhue Blaine (the Author's Father), with Ethel Sally Blaine and Jesse Blaine Crowder, Sisters at Hamilton Field, San Francisco, California Upon Sally's Arrival After Liberation

Photo from the Ethel "Sally" Blaine Millett Collection

Sally in Happier Times After the War

Photo from the Ethel "Sally" Blaine Millett Collection

THE DEFEAT OF EVIL

The Abyss roared and thrashed and fought for its life, but the evil inside was dying. The groaning was now just a hoarse whisper. The darkness of tyranny and thirst for power was overcome with the light of freedom and deliverance. Worldwide, the Axis of Evil was being defeated by the Allied forces, one bloody regime at a time.

EPILOGUE

General Douglas MacArthur kept his promise and returned to the Philippines. When he evacuated himself, his wife, his son, and various household staff from Corregidor to the safe shores of Australia in March 1942, he left US and Filipino troops scratching their heads as to his logic that he could do more good coordinating the war from afar. But he famously said, "I shall return." On October 20, 1944, MacArthur landed on the island of Leyte, centrally located within the Philippine archipelago. To much fanfare and with photographic documentation, he and several of his top aides waded ashore to a group of journalists and radio broadcasters. "People of the Philippines, I have returned!" he declared into the waiting microphones. This press event marked the beginning of the liberation of the Philippines from Japanese occupation. By January of 1945, MacArthur's reinforcements led an invasion of Luzon Island, home of Santo Tomas POW camp and other camps where American and Filipino troops were being held. These maneuvers were seen as the beginning of the defeat of the Japanese by US and Filipino troops. But the prisoners being held at Santo Tomas knew nothing of MacArthur's return until those 44th

Tank Battalion troops demolished the front gate of the Jesuit compound.

MacArthur's return restored the military leadership and troops necessary to defeat the Japanese Imperial forces. It also served as a morale booster for both the Filipino people and the Allied forces in the Pacific. MacArthur was also instrumental in preparing the government of the Philippines for their independence from the United States in 1946.

But only one-third of the men MacArthur left behind survived to see his return.

Sally remembered, throughout the ordeal in the POW camp, that she was needed as part of a humanitarian effort to keep the other internees safe and healthy. The nurses had a purpose, which in turn kept them in better spirits and made them more likely to survive than other POWs at Santo Tomas. Seventy-seven American military nurses were interned at Santo Tomas during WWII. These nurses, known as the "**Angels of Bataan and Corregidor,**" provided care for their patients, regardless of nationality, race, religion, political views, or even the fact that the nurses were held captive by some of those patients. **All of the nurses survived** their time in the Philippines and came home to America after the war.

WWII enthusiasts usually don't talk about **Hirohito** with the same disgust as they do **Adolf Hitler or Benito Mussolini**. Japanese tradition considered the emperor to be divine, and even after the US bombing of Nagasaki and Hiroshima, Hirohito was still revered by his countrymen and women. War-crimes trials didn't direct the execution of the Emperor of Japan for the attack on Pearl Harbor in 1941, which resulted in all-out war with the Allied nations. His **prime minister, Hideki Tojo, was arrested, tried, convicted, and executed** instead, **along with Tojo's top military officers**. **President Harry S. Truman** of the United States **insisted that Hirohito be reinstated as the rightful emperor of Japan**. The country would need a leader who was steady and fair and who would not regret refusing to be part of **the Axis of Evil triad of Hitler, Mussolini,** and himself. Indeed, it was **Hirohito** who determined to end the war in 1945 by **commanding the Japanese people to** "endure the unendurable" and **surrender.** Hirohito lived out the rest of his long life as a beloved, gentle, and rather eccentric butterfly collector.

If Angelito Domingo Orasyon-Del Rosario had been a real person and not perhaps an angel sent from heaven to protect and uphold the nurses of Bataan, Corregidor, and Santo Tomas POW camp, **his mother** may or may not have been killed by the Japanese in the final months of the war to regain the Philippines. One of the most infamous events was the **Manila Massacre in February 1945**, where Japanese troops engaged in a brutal campaign of torture, rape, and mass killings. The **atrocities committed during this period were tried as war crimes**, and Japanese military leaders were held accountable.

When Sally got back to the United States, landing in San Francisco on February 23, 1945, she was met by her brother, Colonel Mayhue D. Blaine (the author's father), who managed to commandeer a United States Army Air Corps plane to pick his sister up. Also on hand to greet Sally upon her return was Sally's sister Jesse Crowder of

Concord, California. Sometime later, when Sally was at a rest and recuperation (R&R) week in Florida, **she met Colonel George Van Millett Jr. (nicknamed Zip).** Colonel Millett, a commander of a Paratroop Regiment during the Normandy Invasion, was held in a POW camp in Germany until the end of WWII. The couple fell in love and **were married**. Because both members of a married couple were not allowed to serve in the US military at that time, Sally was forced to retire early with honors, and Zip remained in the United States Armed Forces. The couple had two sons. When the children were small, and **Zip** was stationed in Lebanon, he **died suddenly**. Leaving the children with friends, Sally accompanied Zip's body to Washington DC, where she was again met by her brother Mayhue Blaine. Zip was **buried at Arlington National Cemetery with full military honors**. Sally returned to Lebanon to move her children back to the United States. She worked for many years as a private duty nurse, with her last residence being San Antonio, Texas. The last time the author spoke to her Aunt Sally by phone was just days before her death.

Ethel "Sally" Blaine Millett died on March 8, 2005, in San Antonio, Texas, at the age of 90. She was **buried with full military honors above her husband,** as is the custom at Arlington National Cemetery where space has become a premium. The funeral was officiated by two female Army Generals.

The world would live in **relative peace for eight decades,** until a new force of **right-wing extremism would rear its ugly head in the world** and **the Abyss** began to hiss again.

Sally Speaking at the White House
Date and Photographer Unknown. *Photo from the Ethel "Sally" Blaine Millett Collection*

ACKNOWLEDGMENTS

They say it takes a village to raise a child, and I would contend it took the world to write this book! That is to say I had help from people from many walks of life and several cultures, a great deal of online information, and my own remembrances of the beautiful, fearless, and talented woman my father's generation called "Ethel," but whom I called "Aunt Sally." I will do my best to give credit to all of you who helped me with this amazing book project, and to try to tell what first drew me to each of you for help in writing this story.

Thanks first and foremost to Ann Millett, widow of my cousin Van (Aunt Sally's son). You got this project started by offering me Aunt Sally's personal effects, because I was an author and no one else in the family seemed to want them! I said, "Yes, please!" And my life had an added purpose...for seven years until I completed the book!

Ann Aubitz, my publisher and longtime friend, for your patience, your creativity, your grasp of my passion for this story, and for your humor. You are a professional who knows her stuff and was not afraid to search out something new for me when I needed it.

The winner of the book naming contest, Michele Hein, who nailed it with the line from the third verse of America the Beautiful, which reads, *"Oh beautiful for heroes proved in liberating strife, who more than self did country love and **mercy more than life."** **Mercy More Than Life** encapsulates how the fearless, dedicated and always professional Angels of Bataan approached their very difficult job of caring for their patients first in open-air hospitals in the jungle and later in a walled university-become-POW-camp. The tag line for the title, **Ethel "Sally" Blaine Millett, WWII Bataan Nurse and Japanese POW**, delineates about whom this book was written.

My "beta" readers who took the time to read my manuscript when it was far from finished, and who gave me helpful and much-needed critiques as well as kudos to keep me going. Susan Schussler, Nicole Fende, and Katherine Barton, you gave me the first (gentle) critiques of my project, all of which helped me craft a more compelling story of my Aunt Sally's amazing journey through World War II.

Women of Words (WOW), the three-hundred-plus women writers' group in the Minneapolis/St. Paul Metro area, chaired by Connie Anderson. So many of you have kept me afloat when I thought my little paper boat would surely sink. I love you all like sisters!

Lindsey Briggs, RN, BSN, ICU nurse at Lakeview Hospital, Stillwater, Minnesota, you cared for me in 2023. You had flown many flights for both Operation Desert Storm and Operation Enduring Freedom, bringing injured service men and women to Walter Reed Hospital in

Washington, DC, for treatment. From you I received invaluable information about critical combat injuries and field treatment, such as those seen in the outdoor jungle hospitals during the Bataan campaign. You lent credibility to my story and helped me "show rather than tell" about wartime nursing.

Christian Balina, Filipino chef and a most useful contributor. You helped me bring Angelito to life as a believable young Filipino man in the midst of impossible circumstances. The minute you read two lines about him, you knew exactly what kind of character I was trying to create. You immediately grasped his role in my book and helped me to craft him in an authentic and convincing way, in his use of the English language as well as his charming personality and impenetrable Christian faith. I am so glad I met you at just the right time.

Chris McDougal at the Museum of the Pacific War, Fredericksburg, Texas, for your help and encouragement when I first began this project. You informed me that Aunt Sally's two-hour oral history was available for use by the public at no charge. I was able to use every word my aunt recorded, which gave me the main storyline and lent a hauntingly sweet and inscrutable tone to the story. And listening to my aunt's voice on the recording brought me right back to my childhood and the larger-than-life Blaine Family Reunions every July in Bible Grove, Missouri. How better to get into the mood to write about my famous aunt?

And above all, I give thanks to God, whose guidance, timing, and grace carried me through every challenge of this journey. I am humbled by His faithfulness and grateful for the strength and inspiration He provided each step of the way.

And last but not least, my "book fans," who have been asking for seven long years, "When will your book about your aunt be done?" Thank you for your enduring patience and support, and thank you for keeping my spirits up in the knowledge at least a few people will still be around to see the book released. Won't we all celebrate then?

Author Meg Blaine Corrigan with Aunt Sally's Photo
Photo by Hilda Birdie from the Meg Blaine Corrigan Collection

ABOUT THE AUTHOR

Meg **Blaine Corrigan** shares stories of wisdom, strength, fear, joy, and risk-taking. A Christian author, speaker, and trainer with over thirty years work experience in the mental health field, Meg holds a master's degree in counseling from the University of New Mexico. Now retired, she imparts her insights to a diverse range of adults and youth in various settings. Meg has four titles in print: *Then I Am Strong: Moving From My Mother's Daughter to God's Child* a memoir abut growing up in an alcoholic home; *Perils of a Polynesian Percussionist*, a novel with stories from her years playing drums in a Hawaiian show band; *Saints With Slingshots One and Two: Daily Devotions for the Slightly Tarnished But Perpetually Forgiven Christian*, two daily devotional books which began life as a popular blog read in over 40 countries by 9000+ people.

One of her proudest achievements is the book she has written using the personal effects of her Aunt Ethel "Sally" Blaine Millett, which she received from Sally's daughter-in-law, as well as the transcript for Sally's oral history. ***Mercy More Than Life: Ethel "Sally" Blaine Millett, WWII Bataan Nurse and Japanese POW*** is a labor of love and a tribute to the incredible woman at the center of this story.

Meg lives at Croixdale Retirement Community in Bayport, Minnesota, with her beloved carousel horse, *Mr. Ed*, a towering artificial coconut palm Plant Friend *Shaka*, and a very special Teddy bear named *Amazing Grace*. Connect with her at www.MegCorrigan.com

BOOK CLUB QUESTIONS

1. The book's first chapter is called The Emperor Had No Choice, and is about the existential choice facing Michinomiya Hirohito, Emperor of Japan at the outset of WWII. Why do you think the author placed this chapter first in the story? Do you think you might have approached the story with a different mindset if the story had begun with Sally's humble beginnings in Bible Grove, Missouri? Why or why not? How does the chapter about Emperor Hirohito's emotional struggles impact the hearing of those humble beginnings of our hero?

2. What is the story's central conflict? Who is involved in it and what is at stake for that character or characters? How does the main character navigate the events she experiences?

3. From whose perspective is the story told? How does that perspective impact the way readers view the story? What do you know about where the story's

perspective comes from? Is the assigned genre of "historical fiction" puzzling to you?

4. Describe the main character, Sally. What are her traits at the beginning of the story? How does she change, or how does she stay true to the way she was, as the story progresses? What scenes showcase her strengths? Show her weaknesses? Reveal her humanity?

5. Why do you think it was necessary to assign the genre of "historical fiction" rather than "historical biography" to this publication? Sally's oral history was relayed in a straightforward manner, excluding many historical facts to help readers know the background and the gravity of the story. Sally also relayed very little dialogue, leaving scenes lacking in plot advancement, tension, emotion, and a more realistic experience for the reader. What was another feature of the book that required abandoning the genre of "historical biography?"

6. The character Angelito Domingo Orasyon-Del Rosario, or just Angelito, is a creation of pure fiction. Why do you believe the author chose to place such a character within Sally's very real story? Is he believable? What is Angelito's purpose in the book? Why do you think the author had him die before the nurses were evacuated from Corregidor? What do you think would have happened to him if he had lived and was forced to make the Bataan Death March? What if he ended up at Santo Tomas? What

would that have been like? If he had lived, do you think he would have continued to "live Christ" throughout the war?

7. Where are the book's climax scenes? Are there more than one? What things change—or do not change—for the characters after those scenes? Are the changes (or lack thereof) believable?

8. Is there a passage that stood out as particularly memorable? Why might that be?

9. What do you think of the book's ending? Is it believable? Satisfying? Disappointing?

10. What knowledge did you have about this story prior to reading the book? Do you think the phrase "The Other Pearl Harbor" is justified? Why or why not? Did the book educate you on what took place in the Philippines during WWII? Would you be likely to share some of this story with others in your life? Why or why not?